"I wish I could turn my scars into something beautiful like yours."

"You are beautiful," he whispered, his gaze sweeping the length of her.

"How can this be beautiful?" she asked, flicking her hand at her scarred face and arm.

"It's beautiful because you are, and the scars are a beautiful reminder that you survived and thrived despite what someone else inflicted on you. Don't ever, ever tell yourself you're anything but beautiful."

If only that were possible, Marlise thought. He might say she was beautiful, but a man like Cal Newfellow would never consider her a romantic companion. Her scars went far deeper than her skin, and sometimes those scars were harder to hide.

D0802276

THE PERFECT WITNESS

KATIE METTNER

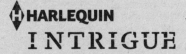

If you purchased this book without a cover you should be aware that this book is stolen property. It was reported as "unsold and destroyed" to the publisher, and neither the author nor the publisher has received any payment for this "stripped book."

For Linda

Thank you for believing in me when I didn't believe in myself. The memories of your loving encouragement in every aspect of my life are the reason I had the courage to make *our* dream a reality. Wherever you are over the rainbow, I still love ya more.

H HARLEQUIN®
INTRIGUE™

Recycling programs for this product may not exist in your area.

ISBN-13: 978-1-335-59148-7

The Perfect Witness

Copyright © 2024 by Katie Mettner

All rights reserved. No part of this book may be used or reproduced in any manner whatsoever without written permission except in the case of brief quotations embodied in critical articles and reviews.

This is a work of fiction. Names, characters, places and incidents are either the product of the author's imagination or are used fictitiously. Any resemblance to actual persons, living or dead, businesses, companies, events or locales is entirely coincidental.

For questions and comments about the quality of this book, please contact us at CustomerService@Harlequin.com.

Harlequin Enterprises ULC
22 Adelaide St. West, 41st Floor
Toronto, Ontario M5H 4E3, Canada
www.Harlequin.com

Printed in U.S.A.

Katie Mettner wears the title of "the only person to lose her leg after falling down the bunny hill" and loves decorating her prosthetic leg to fit the season. She lives in Northern Wisconsin with her own happily-ever-after and wishes for a dog now that her children are grown. Katie has an addiction to coffee and Twitter and a lessening aversion to Pinterest—now that she's quit trying to make the things she pins.

Books by Katie Mettner

Harlequin Intrigue

Secure One

Going Rogue in Red Rye County
The Perfect Witness

Visit the Author Profile page at Harlequin.com.

CAST OF CHARACTERS

Cal Newfellow—As a security expert, he excels at keeping people safe. As a man, he has enough experience to know safety is an illusion.

Marlise—As the star witness against her ex-boss, she's in hiding until her trial. She has secrets she's told no one, and they're the reason she's being hunted.

The Miss—She's MIA, but she wants Marlise. The secrets she thought would die in Red Rye were about to be revealed, and she couldn't let that happen.

Charlotte—Defecting on a mission for The Miss was a death sentence, but it was a chance she had to take.

Mack Holbock—Cal's right-hand man at Secure One. He'd fought alongside Cal and Roman in the army, but now Secure One is the only country he serves. He just needs a chance to prove his worth, even if that means breaking orders.

Roman Jacobs—Married to the other key witness in The Madame's trial, he knew they had to find The Miss if they wanted to live happily-ever-after.

Mina Jacobs—Tortured by The Miss in Red Rye, would she go undercover to root her out and bring her to justice?

Chapter One

"Meanwhile, in Minneapolis, the trial for Cynthia Moore, aka The Madame, the famed head of a sex trafficking empire, is underway after a lengthy eighteen-month delay. The extensive evidence for the case was nearly insurmountable for both the prosecution and the defense. The trial is expected to last several weeks while the jury remains sequestered. Later today, the defense will put a woman on the stand who was in charge of the household at the Red Rye escort house before it burned. That witness, whom courts are only identifying as Marlise, is expected to testify against her former boss, Cynthia Moore, while revealing what she knew about other illegal activities under The Madame's eye. Former FBI agent Mina Jacobs, the undercover agent sent in to find evidence of prostitution, is expected to testify after Marlise. Jacobs's testimony is expected to take several days, considering her connection to her then boss, and Cynthia Moore's husband, David Moore."

Marlise's gaze flicked to the screen as her heart

rate crept up to near heart attack level. She was waiting for Cal to pick her up for the drive to the courthouse. Secure One was three hours away from the city, so they'd all driven in last night and stayed at a hotel. Cal didn't like it, but realistically, they had no choice. With The Miss still on the run, everyone was worried she'd pick today to tag them. Marlise knew it was a real possibility, but if she made it to the courthouse today and gave her testimony, The Miss would have no reason to hunt her. Unless she wanted revenge. If that were the case, Marlise would never be safe or free.

"We've asked our law expert to break down the case for us," the newscaster continued. "He is in no way affiliated with the case but can offer insight into both the defense and the prosecution's plan of attack. Thanks for being here, Barry."

"It's my pleasure," a man in a tweed suit said. He was sitting in an office on a blue couch, and the windows behind him gave the audience a view of the Minneapolis skyline lit with a thousand sparkling lights. It was early, and the sun wasn't up, but that didn't mean the city was quiet. That was one thing Marlise hated about the city. The dark. It hid the worst side of humanity, and she'd experienced the worst side of humanity enough times in her short life to fear it. She preferred the quiet solitude of Secure One, where she worked keeping Cal's men fed every day. Whenever she was scared or nervous, she could walk out to the lake and watch the water ripple while taking deep breaths. Cal's property lent itself to isolation and made you forget the outside world existed. Marlise had lived on the streets for years, and no one knew what a jungle they were more than her, so she appreciated being wrapped in a womb of safety and protection at Secure One.

"There is no perfect witness," the lawyer said when she tuned back in to the news program. "Both sides will find something to use against any witness. A small misstep, a social media post or even an image taken out of context can throw doubt into the minds of the jurors. You have to remember that the prosecution has to prove beyond a reasonable doubt that crimes were committed, but all the defense has to do is prove reasonable doubt that the defendant is innocent. Each side will look for any chink in the witness's armor before putting them on the stand."

A shiver ran down Marlise's spine. *There is no such thing as a perfect witness.* Was that true? She still had to try. She had to do her part to put The Madame and her husband behind bars. She refused to acknowledge the woman's real name. She would always be The Madame, a badge of shame for the damage she'd done to girls like her. Yes, The Miss was still out there, but Marlise had to start where she had a little bit of power and control. Her entire life had been about lack of control, and she was tired of it.

Living and working at Secure One had changed her. She was stronger, both physically and emotionally. When Mina was kidnapped by The Madame, she had hurt her foot beyond repair and, because of that, was now an amputee. Marlise watched her come back from that stronger and more determined to make a difference in the world. Mina's fighting spirit inspired Marlise's.

Absently, she rubbed the leathery skin on her arm. She had healed from the extensive burns she'd endured at the house in Red Rye, but the nerve damage and disfigurement were still hard to live with some days. Cal had insisted that his nurse, Selina, treat her skin with a gel to care for the disorder better, which was something she could never afford on her own. The skin felt better with each passing day, and she had hope that it might lessen the burning pain even more. When she'd first woken up in the hospital after the fire, she'd wished she'd died there rather than be alive inside her burning body. Her heart paused in her chest when memories of that day came rushing back to her.

"I heard them talking. They know you're an FBI agent. You're not getting out of here alive, Agent August."

The woman Marlise had come to see as her only friend in the house hesitated before a shaky smile lifted her lips. Marlise turned back to the mixer, the cookie dough swirling around inside the bowl while terror swirled through her gut. She worried about what would happen next if her friend actually was an undercover FBI agent. Would she be arrested? Marlise wanted to throw up at the thought. She was just the cook! She wasn't involved with the escort service. At least she wasn't anymore. They could still say she was or at least say she knew about it and should have reported it. She knew better, though. Red Rye was like fight club. That was the only rule.

At least she had Agent August. Maybe she'd tell the authorities that Marlise didn't go out on dates the way the other girls did. She swallowed over the nervous lump in her throat. Her life was about to change again, and she wasn't ready. She wasn't ready to go back to the streets.

"Thanks for this, Marlise," Agent August said as she snagged a cookie from the tray with a wave.

Marlise didn't react. She didn't look at her or do anything until she was gone. Then she calmly turned and pulled out another pan of cookies from the oven.

"What does your gut say about the agent who was undercover there?" the newscaster asked, bringing Marlise back to the present. "Wouldn't she be considered the perfect witness?"

"No," the lawyer insisted as Marlise's attention snapped back to the television. "Again, there is no perfect witness. The defense will try to discredit the agent. They'll say her boss at the FBI, former special agent David Moore, who is also The Madame's husband as you'll recall, put her there unknowingly, but she was there long enough to find a smoking gun. She was injured while undercover and again while arresting David Moore. The defense will try to convince the jury that she's got a vendetta against the Moores now."

"Could you blame her? I don't know anyone who wouldn't feel intense hatred toward the people responsible for their torture and attempted murder."

"On the human nature side of the case, that will play well for her, but it could harm her on the legal side of the case."

"The same can be said for Marlise?"

"Absolutely. Of course, Marlise is a victim of The Madame, and on the human nature side of the case, she will be a stellar witness, but they will find something to discredit her. It will be harder with her since her past was wiped away, but if they have to, they'll twist something perfectly reasonable into something ugly."

Marlise flicked the television off, disgusted with how the media had turned The Madame's trial into a sideshow. She knew firsthand that it wasn't a sideshow for the girls in those houses. The human nature side of those houses was a terrifying way to live while constantly worrying about dying. It tossed her right back to that day, and the swirling in her mind dropped her to the bed.

A thud. A muffled scream. Another thud. A moan of agony. Why didn't the FBI come and help her friend? Where were they? Marlise had noticed Agent August tap out a message on her phone before she left the kitchen.

Do you want to be here when they show up? that little voice asked. *It's time to make like a tree and leave.*

The voice was right, and she had to do it now. She scurried to her room, another thud from overhead bringing her shoulders up to her ears. Marlise waited for the scream from her friend to follow, but this time, the house stayed silent. She ran down the hallway now, her feet swift. It was only then that she realized the other girls weren't in the house. She swallowed around the truth that clogged her throat. They didn't care what happened to her. The other girls were cash cows for the organization, but she was disposable. She always had been.

Her gaze swept her tiny room for someone waiting for her, but it was empty. She reached for her backpack and hesitated. She should only take her money. No bag to slow her down or make it evident that she was running. She pulled out a wad of one-hundred-dollar bills from under her mattress with a grim smile. It wouldn't get her far, but it would get her out of Red Rye. She grabbed a jacket and threw it on, stashing the money in a secret pocket.

The Miss's words ran through her mind. "I'm taking the girls and getting out before the FBI breaks down our door. Only the moneymakers. Yes. No. She's dead weight to me now. I don't need her. I think she knew all along the FBI were involved."

Marlise didn't know her friend was an FBI agent, but she wasn't sticking around to get the same kind of treatment Agent August was suffering. Another *thud, another scream, and then something tickled her nose. She sniffed.*

Smoke.

The cookies were burning! Too bad. Marlise wasn't going back to the kitchen. They could be waiting for her there. She hoped the smoke would distract them and give Agent August a reprieve. Marlise had to get out before she couldn't. If they stopped her, they'd kill her. She had to get out of Red Rye, but she had one more thing to do. She hated to waste precious time on it, but if she didn't stop for her treasure, the proof would be gone for good.

Run, her brain told her feet, but she forced herself to enter the hallway at a normal pace. Smoke filled the space, and she realized nothing was normal. It wasn't her cookies burning. The house was on fire, and she had to get out! Choking on the acrid smoke, she got as low as possible and kept her hand on the wall. She was desperate for fresh air as the cloying thickness choked her, tempting her to open her lungs to it. It wanted to work its tentacles through her until she followed it down into the bowels of hell.

She wouldn't. She couldn't. She needed to get out of this house alive, or everything Agent August had worked for would be lost. If they ever caught The Madame, she'd have the evidence to help put her away for good.

There was a knock on the hotel room door, and she jumped. Her heart rate, already up from being trapped in the memories of Red Rye, kicked up another notch until she heard his voice.

"Mary."

Cal.

He'd started calling her Mary last summer when she'd moved back to Secure One to work for him. She hadn't used the name in a decade, but he insisted on using it when they were alone together. She wasn't sure why. She'd ask, but she was too afraid of the answer. Cal held power over her life, whether it was intended or not. He kept her employed, housed and fed while they awaited the trial, but there was more to it. He sheltered her—both physically and emotionally.

She checked to make sure it was him before she opened the door. He was inside the room with the door closed before she saw him move. He was that way. Even at six foot four inches tall, two hundred and fifty pounds of muscle and with tats covering both arms, he moved like a ghost. Cal was always intense, but this morning, he was laser focused on the details as he prepared her for the trip to the courthouse.

He slung a bag onto the bed and started pulling out items. "Mina and Roman are preparing the cars. It's time to get dressed for court."

Marlise glanced down at her pants and long-sleeve blouse. "I am dressed for court."

"Correction," he said, handing her a black jacket. "For the drive to court."

She took the jacket, but her eyes widened when he

pulled out a bulletproof vest. "Don't you think that's going a bit far, Cal?"

"If anything, it's not going far enough, but it's all we have, so put it on."

Marlise had learned when Cal issued an order, he expected you to follow it. He lowered it over her head and then tightened the side straps down.

"I should have gotten a child's size. You swim in this thing."

"If they make child-sized bulletproof vests, I don't want to be part of humanity," she muttered.

He cocked a brow at her, and she sighed. Of course, they made them. Cal held up a small walkie-talkie and attached it to her vest before he helped her cover the vest with her jacket. "The walkie-talkie will only contact the other people on our network." Marlise nodded, but she swallowed over the fear in her throat when he turned away. She could see in his dark brown eyes that he was scared too. If Cal was scared, there was a good chance she could die today.

When he turned back to her, he handed her a small handgun and showed her the full magazine before popping it back into the gun. "You can't take this into the courthouse, obviously, but until then, it stays within reach."

She grabbed his hand before he could tuck the gun into the front of her vest. "That doesn't look familiar."

"It's just like our training guns, but it shoots live ammunition. Remember, the safety is on the trigger.

Don't aim. Just point and shoot. And while you're shooting, run."

"Cal, this feels a bit overboard for a fifteen-minute drive to the courthouse."

"Maybe, maybe not," he said with a clenched jaw. "If The Miss is out there, and she's worried about what you'll say on the stand, she knows exactly where you will be and when."

"We don't even know if she's still in the country. It's been radio silence for years, Cal."

He grabbed her packed backpack off the bed and slung it over his shoulder. "That doesn't mean she's not in play. I've worked too hard to keep you alive the last year to take any chances on the one-yard line. Mina is dressed to look like you and will be riding with Roman. I'll be driving the other SUV with you in the back."

"It's not smart to put Mina at risk, Cal. She has to testify too."

"We're making it look like we're bringing you in one at a time. If my car is empty, they'll think on a passing glance that Mina is you. They're trained agents with more years under their belts combined than you've been alive, so don't worry about Mina and Roman. We'll get you to the courthouse safely, and once we do, you're one step closer to living your life free of The Madame."

Cal walked to the door and checked the peephole before radioing down to Roman and Mina in the underground garage. He was right. The media had broadcast loud and clear when she was testifying at the trial. It had been on the evening news a week ago, and she wouldn't forget that scene anytime soon. Cal had been so angry he'd thrown his coffee cup against the wall before he walked out of the control room and disappeared for an hour. Roman had assured her that his brother was just frustrated with the media turning the trial into a circus and putting people's lives at risk, but she still carried guilt about it. If Roman hadn't gone to Cal for help when he found Mina, Cal would never have met Marlise, and his life wouldn't be so complicated.

Mina told her she couldn't think that way because Cal didn't, but it was days like today that she wasn't so sure. As much as it pained her to think about leaving Secure One, and this man, she wouldn't have a choice if she made it through today. They both deserved to be free.

CAL BRAKED AT the exit to the parking garage. Roman had just pulled out with Mina in the passenger side dressed as Marlise. With a wig down over her face and a pair of sunglasses, Mina could pull it off. He didn't like putting his brother in the position of risking his wife, but she was a former FBI agent and could hold her own. Two years ago, his brother showed up on his doorstep with his compromised partner in tow. Mina had been on the run from a woman they called The Madame for a year, but she was desperate for protection and a chance to heal.

He was convinced Secure One could take care of her. He'd naively believed he had all the safeguards on his property to protect them, but he soon learned nothing was further from the truth. The Madame's men infiltrated his borders and took Mina right out from under their noses. They got her back, but he'd learned some hard lessons that day, and he wasn't giving anyone another chance to attack his home or his people.

One of those people was in his back seat dressed in bulletproof armor, and he hoped this ruse would work long enough to get her to the courthouse. Marlise used to live in the Red Rye house, an escort service and modern-day brothel, run by The Madame. She was also Mina's only friend on the inside. When that house burned to the ground, with Marlise still inside it, The Miss and The Madame thought they'd mitigated a threat. They were wrong. Marlise knew things no one else did, and that was why The Miss could be waiting to ambush them on their route. She was a dangerous, invisible woman, but the chances she'd become visible today were almost 100 percent.

Truthfully, he didn't know if she was even in business anymore, but the part of him that had done bad things in the name of helping good people told him she would soon turn up. The Miss was hunting for the last two people who could identify her. In the eyes of The Miss, Marlise was a nobody, but she also knew more about the operation than even Mina did. The Miss didn't want either woman spilling the beans about what went on in Red Rye, but she would see Marlise as an easy snatch and grab. Worst-case scenario, she was willing to shut her up any way she could, including with a bullet from a distance. He wouldn't let that happen.

"Are you okay back there?" he asked, waiting for his turn to leave the parking garage.

"Snug as a bug," she replied sarcastically, and he snorted.

"I know it's uncomfortable, but it's better this way."

"If you say so."

Cal slid his sunglasses across his face and followed his brother down the street. Following his brother defined his life. The moment Roman joined the army, Cal never considered doing anything else. He signed up at seventeen. At eighteen, Cal followed his brother into special training for the military police. By nineteen, he was the youngest member of the Special Reaction Team at Fort McCoy. They'd called him "kid," but Cal didn't mind. He knew why he was there. To do the job. Protect his country. To stand next to his brother again. His team may have teased him about being a kid, but they knew he wasn't one. They had each other's back every time and all the time until that one time.

People always said blood was thicker than water, but not when it came to Cal Newfellow and Roman Jacobs. They may not share a last name, but they shared a bond that went deeper. They grew up together as best friends and foster brothers, but Roman never treated him like a kid. Over the last decade, Roman looked to his little brother for help more often than not. When Mina had gone missing, driven into hiding by The Madame after their undercover operation went south, Cal helped Roman find her. They complemented each other's strengths and weaknesses, and that made them an effective team.

That was the reason Roman and Mina left the FBI last year to be part of Secure One. Roman's extensive combat training had made his men sharper, stronger and more advanced in self-defense and combat fighting than half the guys in the military. Mina's skills at a computer kept his security business running smoothly. Over the last year, she had stopped two cyberattacks aimed at several of his VIP clients.

On days like today, he was glad to be working with his brother again. Cal had done enough bad things in his life. Now his goal was to do good things to better the world. He blew out a breath as he checked all the mirrors of the SUV. He had to stay sharp. He had a witness to protect.

Is she just a witness though?

That is all she can be, he reminded himself.

Marlise had arrived at Secure One broken, in pain and terrified. He'd made sure she healed better than anyone could have predicted. Once she had her strength back, he trained her in self-defense and gun safety. While she could bake a mean chocolate chip cookie, she also had deadly aim with a firearm. He got off on giving her back power over her life. He hoped that she could find newfound freedom once this trial was over. He wanted her to stay at Secure One, but he understood she'd been bought and paid for over the last decade. Hell, her name wasn't even Marlise. It was Mary.

Cal shook his head and readjusted his focus on the road. Fifteen miles separated them and the courthouse, and he had to get her there in one piece. He reminded himself to send a thank-you to the media and their useless mouths. Now was the time to attack if The Miss wanted to throw the entire trial into chaos and get away a free woman. If she tried hard enough, she could get a twofer with Mina without even knowing it. He could feel the evil coming. The hair on the back of his neck was electric and fear crackled in his chest.

"Do you think there's such a thing as a perfect witness?" Marlise asked from the back seat.

"Absolutely not. Humans are imperfect, so it's relatively easy to discredit a witness. Why do you ask?" Cal asked, waiting at a red light.

Roman was third in line, and he hoped his brother remembered they both had to clear the green light, so they didn't get separated. Cal hated driving through the concrete jungle with a witness as hot as Marlise, but he had no choice. If they hadn't stayed over last night, the drive would have been three hours long, and by the time they reached the city, they wouldn't be sharp or reactive. Unfortunately, the city made escape routes challenging to plan, and he always felt like a caged animal trapped by the street grids with no easy way out.

"I heard a lawyer on the news say no witness is perfect. The newscaster asked about Mina, and the lawyer said the defense would claim she stayed in Red Rye too long and should have had the evidence sooner."

Cal pressed down the accelerator to clear the yellow light. "I'm sure they'll throw anything at the wall and hope it sticks, but we know none of it is true. Mina never had the evidence because her boss was pulling the strings to keep her there."

"It made me think that I might be the perfect witness."

"I don't follow."

"Think about it, Cal," Marlise said. "Thanks to David Moore, my past before I moved into the Red Rye house is gone. There's nothing for the defense to dig up."

"That's true, but everyone is vulnerable," he reminded her. "They can twist simple things to make you look bad."

"It would be hard to discredit someone held against their will."

"They'll simply say you were free to leave at any time."

"I wasn't though!" Marlise hissed. "I wasn't. You know I couldn't leave. If I left, they'd have killed me." He heard the terror of those years in her whispered words. Cal wanted to pull the car over and gather

her in his arms to protect her. That was a reaction he'd had a lot since she'd first stepped foot on his plane, injured and scared. A reaction he didn't like. He reminded himself his only job was to get her to the courthouse to testify. Once that was over, they could part ways and go on with their lives independently of each other.

That little voice inside his head laughed.

"Deep breaths, Mary," he encouraged, his focus still on the back of Roman's SUV. They were ten minutes out now. "We know you couldn't leave, but the defense will try to throw doubt into the jurors' minds any way they can. That's their job. It's widely accepted that women who are sex trafficked into those houses aren't there by choice. It's the prosecutor's job to explain that to the jury. You just have to relax, okay? You're not going to be charged with a crime. I won't allow it."

"I don't know if even your steely determination can outpower The Miss," she whispered. "But, just in case something happens, thank you for taking care of me the last few years and getting me this far. You didn't have to do it, but I would be dead already if you hadn't let me stay at Secure One."

"I'm going to get you there safely, Mary. Don't give up on me now," he begged.

"I'm not," she assured him. The sound of Velcro being unstrapped reached his ears. "I've got my gun, and I know how to use it, thanks to you."

His lips broke into a grin that made him glad that

neither she nor his team could see it. "Mary, it has been my greatest honor to be part of your life. You don't need to thank me for anything. Just get up on that stand and put these people away. I'm proud of you and your tenacity, so let's cross the finish line. We're in go time."

Marlise knew what that meant. He heard her take a deep breath before she went silent. He punched a button on the dash that connected him to Roman's car. "Five and in. What do you see?"

"Road construction up ahead. Slow traffic."

Cal hissed out a cuss word before he responded. "There was no planned construction anywhere on the route."

He heard Roman's laughter before he answered. "As if the city of Minneapolis cares?"

He was silent, and Cal waited for an update as they crawled forward. Since Roman was the lead car, he would have to be the one to assess the scene.

"Utility work. Looks like a city truck. We're fine. Just go slow around them."

"Six and in now," Cal said, updating them on the GPS arrival time.

He wasn't happy about the added minute. Extra seconds could mean lives, and the one he was carrying was a life he'd worked hard to save for reasons he refused to address. He might bury his head in the sand about how he felt for the tiny woman in the back seat, but he would never give up on keeping her safe.

Roman's SUV skirted the truck with ease, but

Cal's bigger vehicle would be a tight squeeze, so he slowed to pass the truck. "Almost there," he said to keep Marlise calm.

There was laughter from the back seat. "No, we aren't, but nice try, Newfellow."

As he approached the truck, his lips turned up in a grin, but his amusement quickly disappeared when the scene before him registered. The truck wasn't from the City of Minneapolis. The last time he checked, they didn't arm their city employees with automatic rifles.

"Stay down!" he yelled as the first bullet collided with the side of the SUV.

Marlise's scream filled his ears as he yanked the car to the right and slammed into the parked truck in an attempt to unbalance the shooters. He didn't wait to see if it worked before throwing the SUV into Reverse and slamming his foot down on the accelerator. He should have listened to that hair on the back of his neck. It had never let him down.

Chapter Two

"Cal!" Marlise yelled from the back seat, where she hid under a heavy black blanket. She no sooner got the word out than the SUV lurched and nearly threw her to the floor. She had a seat belt around her waist, and she threw her hand out to brace against Cal's seat. "I'll return fire!"

Before she could, his words chilled her to the bone. "Stay under that blanket, Mary! We're outnumbered, and they have way more firepower!"

Another bullet slammed against the SUV's window, and the bulletproof glass cracked. Marlise tossed the blanket off her head and noticed the front passenger-side window was also hit.

"Cal!" Roman's voice on the radio filled the car as the utility truck rammed them from behind. "Evade! Evade! There are more waiting ahead. We're going left! Do not go to the courthouse! They know you have Marlise!"

A barrage of bullets hit the car, and this time, Cal must have slammed the accelerator because the car jerked, the tires spun, and then they were flying across the city streets, barely avoiding oncoming traffic. All she could do was pray no innocent people got hurt because of her. Marlise wrapped one arm in the seat belt and held her gun in the other. She was ready to defend their lives if it came down to it. That was the least she could do for this man after everything he'd done for her.

"Scatter plan!" Cal yelled.

"Ten-four," Roman answered, and then the radio went silent.

Cal muttered a string of cuss words that would make any girl blush, but she noticed that he didn't slow down. A terrified pit had opened in her belly, and she wanted to cry, but she refused. She would not let The Miss win this time! A bullet slammed into the back window, and then another one tagged the rear door.

"Hold on! We don't stand a chance if I can't lose them!"

"I'm returning fire!" she yelled, but the window refused to budge when she hit the button.

"No!" He yelled the word in anger as he twisted the wheel hard to the left. "If you stick your head out, you're dead. Stay down!"

The words weren't out of his mouth when another bullet smacked the back of the SUV. They'd managed to damage the glass to the point if they got a clear shot, a few more rounds would shatter it. Marlise's arm burned from being twisted in the seat belt, but she didn't have time to worry about it. Sirens had filled the air, and she was worried more people would get hurt because of her.

"Hang on!" Cal yelled to her. "We're using the cops as cover and going off-road!"

"Cal, we're in the city!"

"No choice. Hang on!"

The SUV jumped and metal grated on the undercarriage before they fishtailed, landed hard and straightened out.

"What's your plan, Cal?"

"Once we're clear, we have to find a new vehicle and work our way back to the gathering point so Secure One can extract us."

He fell silent as the SUV hurtled down a bumpy surface while she was rocked back and forth like a boat. A boat!

"What about the river?" she asked, throwing the blanket off her face, securing her gun back in her vest and preparing to unbuckle her seat belt when he stopped. She had memorized the same plans Cal and Roman had and knew exactly what steps to follow.

The bullets had stopped coming for now, but that didn't mean more weren't waiting for them up ahead. "If we could find a boat, we could use the river to get out of the city and closer to Secure One."

"We'd still need a car," he muttered. "We can't take the river any further than St. Cloud."

"At least we wouldn't be here!" she exclaimed, her

voice holding all the fear bubbling up in her belly despite trying to remain calm.

"If the opportunity presents itself, I'm not against it," he said as they bounced over something that made a grinding sound under the car. "Get ready. I'm about to dump this in a grove of trees, and we're going to bail. Grab the go bags!"

She leaned over the back of the seat and grabbed the two black backpacks. Her arm burned, but she ignored it to focus on the plan. After hauling them onto the seat, she unbuckled her seat belt and braced her feet on the front seat until Cal slowed the car and threw it into Park. It had barely lurched to a stop before they were out and running for the trees along the river.

Engulfed by green branches, Cal weaved through them, and she knew he expected her to follow without question. She was grateful for the strength and stamina workouts Cal insisted she do, but the longer they ran, the heavier she breathed. Cal was pulling her along behind him now, and she went down to one knee, his arm pulling hers taut for a moment until he turned back.

"I need a break," she said, her chest aching from carrying the pack and the heavy vest.

He leaned toward her, scooped her up and started running again. "We need more distance between them and us," he huffed as she held on around his neck.

Marlise jumped in his arms. "I have to testify! You have to take me back!"

"That ship sailed, Mary," he said, his breath coming harder now that he was carrying her. "There's no way you're getting near that place. If we're lucky, the cops pick up some of The Miss's women, and they lead them to her."

"And if they don't?"

"Then this doesn't end until someone roots her out of her hole and kills her."

"Stop and put me down!" she ordered. She held her demand in her gaze when Cal glanced down at her. Eventually, his pace slowed, and then he stopped next to a large tree trunk and lowered her back to the ground. "Thank you." Marlise straightened her vest, stiffened her spine and lifted her chin high.

"We can't stop for long. We have no idea if anyone followed us, and the SUV isn't exactly hidden. I don't even trust the cops at this point."

"Understood, but you have to think smart, Cal. You told Roman to follow the scatter plan, which means we do too."

His hand went into his hair as his chest heaved. "I was prepared for an assault, but my heart is still pounding. I can't believe they tried to take us out that close to the courthouse."

"It was their only choice," Marlise said, her trained eye searching the shoreline past the trees. "They didn't know what direction we'd be coming from, but they knew once we funneled down into the hot zone, there would be only so many choices we could make."

Another cuss word fell from his lips, and she bit

back a smile. Men were so transparent, even when they thought they were big bad security agents. "We need to distance ourselves from that mess."

"They're going to be looking for us, Cal. I'm one of their star witnesses."

"You're not going near the courthouse right now. The FBI should have done their job and found The Miss before the trial!"

Marlise rested her hand on his giant forearm. "Cal, take a deep breath. I understand that I can't go there now. We have to get out of here since the prosecution will be on the hunt for their star witness. Besides, we were the ones who decided not to use the FBI for protection."

"Not true," he said with a shake of his head. "They were supposed to be part of the transport team for you. That was why we were in the hotel this morning."

"You never told me that," she said, planting her hand on her hip.

Cal took his hat off and wiped his brow before putting it back on. "It was need-to-know information, and I didn't want you to worry. Ultimately, it was still Secure One that was protecting you. The FBI just wanted a hand in getting their witness to the courthouse. They were in the air as well as waiting on the surrounding streets."

"Then where the hell were they when we needed them?" she demanded. It made her angry that even surrounded by the FBI she wasn't safe.

"I don't know," he admitted with a puff of air.

"That's what scares me about this. We need to get back to Secure One and get Roman and Mina on the official wire with them."

"How did the FBI miss this?"

"Maybe they didn't," he said, cocking a brow.

"No. There's no way the agency still has someone in play, Cal. It's been years since David Moore was arrested, and Mina said everyone in the field office went under a microscope before they were allowed to continue working."

"Sure, in Minneapolis. That doesn't mean every office worker and agent in the FBI was looked at under a lens. Remember, money talks."

"What are we going to do, Cal?" she asked, anxiety filling her.

He tipped her chin up to force eye contact. "We're going to stay alive. Are you ready to run again?"

"We could run, but we need to conserve our energy, Cal. The scatter plan says we find a way back any way we can. We can't use one vehicle longer than an hour before finding another. Gloves must be worn at all times, and the last five miles to the extraction zone has to be approached on foot." Marlise took pleasure in the way his mouth dropped open when she finished the instructions.

"You memorized the scatter plan."

She stepped up to him, chest to chest, and poked herself in the vest. "Of course, I did. It's my life on the line. I've been in life-or-death situations more times than I want to count, Cal. I know how to live and hide on the streets. You'd do well to remember that."

A smile tugged at his lips, and he wrapped his arms around her, giving her a brief hug. Marlise languished in it, glad to be in his arms again in a way that wasn't scary. She would never admit to his face that she was terrified, but she had been for days. There was never any doubt that if The Miss were still out there somewhere, she would look for her at the trial. At this moment, she just needed to feel safe, and his arms always did that for her.

When he released her, he straightened her vest and ensured her gun was secure. "I would never discount your experience, Mary. But this is an urban jungle, and we have few choices but to run."

Marlise motioned him closer to the edge of the tree line along the riverbank and then squatted down. Cal knelt next to her, and she made an arc with her arm as it swung out to the left. It stopped on a bobbing speck on the bank of the river. "That's our run target."

"How did you even see that?" he asked, pulling her up to standing again.

"The Jolly Green Giant was carrying me, and the light glinted off it and into my eye."

Marlise took great pleasure in his snicker as he shook his head. "I'll let you get away with that once." His brow furrowed, but she saw the smile tugging at his lips. "It looks like we're about three miles out from the boat. Let's move."

Cal grabbed her hand and headed deeper into the trees again. She knew he would wind his way there rather than attempt the path of least resistance. He was always looking for a secondary path if their first one was blocked. She matched her steps to his, hard as it was, so she didn't let him down. Marlise would follow him anywhere, but she'd also be ready to defend herself if she had to. He'd said it himself; they were in the concrete jungle now, but she knew that life like the back of her scarred hand.

CAL KNELT, and Marlise slid down his back as she did the same. They'd reached the end of the trees near the back of a property on the Mississippi. There were multiple boats and kayaks tied up to a dock, but he had his eye on just one. A brown Jon boat. It was built for the waters of the Mississippi. He'd had enough experience with them in the service to know their capabilities.

"I need to do some recon before we make any decisions."

"We don't have time to use military strategy, Cal," she hissed from behind him.

He spun and took a knee, grabbing her shoulders so she didn't tip over. "We don't have time not to, Mary. For all we know, that house is full of people! There could be cameras anywhere on that property. We can't waltz in and take a boat if we don't know what we're waltzing into."

He felt her defiance wane as he held her. "Fine, but I'm going with you."

"You don't know the first thing about recon, Mary. While I'm gone, you have a job. Listen and look. You've got the bird call?" She nodded and dug it out of one of her pockets. "Good. You're my eyes from up here. If you see or hear anything, blow that call, then get hidden and stay hidden. Remember the sound of the drones at Secure One?" he asked, and she nodded again. "Listen for that sound. It's unlikely they'd send them this far down the river, but the police will be searching for us eventually. Understood?"

"Got it. I'm not helpless, Cal. Go."

A cuss word slipped out when he ran his sentence back through his head. "We can't go for the boat."

"Why?" she asked. Her question sounded frustrated, but Cal heard the fear and fatigue hiding under it.

"Drones. I can hide you from anyone on land in the center of that boat, but not from the air." Her face fell, and he swore a blue streak internally. "I'm still going to go check the place out. We may not have a choice." He double-checked his gun and turned to her. "Stay alert. Keep your head on a swivel. When I'm ready for you to join me, I'll blow the bird call."

He winked before he headed to the left of her and down a steep embankment. A quick flick of his wristwatch told him it had been two hours since the first bullets flew. He wouldn't hear from Roman again unless he could send out a text. No voice communication could be risked, so he had switched his walkie-talkie off when they'd stopped the first time. When he got back to Mary, he'd check the phone in her pack for a message. It was silent and untraceable, but, with any luck, Mack would have an extraction plan in place.

Cal knew Roman and Mina were fine. The Miss's gang saw right through their plan to keep Marlise hidden and went for his SUV. He kicked himself for not realizing that was a dead giveaway. He and Roman had hoped that the flak jacket and double car entourage to the courthouse would fool them, but they were only fooling themselves.

How could he have been so stupid? Mary could have died today! Cal's steps faltered, and he nearly fell down the slope headfirst. His breathing was ragged, so he took a second to slow his heart rate and calm his breathing. He prided himself on being a ghost, but he felt like a bumbling oaf right now. His focus was split between getting them to safety and how close they came to death today.

Focus. Slow. Steady. Look for signs of life. Are there dogs? Where are the cameras?

The questions forced him to concentrate, and he picked his way down the embankment, avoiding sticks and leaves that could alert a homeowner or a dog. Autumn had arrived in Minnesota, and the dry, fallen leaves weren't doing him any favors. He paused at the bottom of the hill, knelt and let his gaze travel the eaves of the house. They would have to avoid the area if the house had cameras. He saw none at the back of the building, which didn't make sense. They had nearly a quarter of a million dollars' worth of boats at the dock, and they weren't monitoring them?

Sliding along the side of the garage, Cal peeked inside a window. It was empty of cars, but that didn't mean no one was inside the house. Another few feet, and he could stick his head around the side of the garage. His trained eye took in the uncut lawn, the wilting summer flowers, and the front porch swing wrapped to protect it from the winter weather. He ducked back and let out a breath. It looked to be a weekend and summer cabin, but with no cameras on the property, that meant one thing—the boats themselves were protected from theft.

Even if he could break through one of the security devices with his limited tools, he had to face the truth. It wasn't safe on the water. It left them far too exposed, especially in the daylight. A boat battle was nasty business, and Marlise didn't have the experience to live through a gunfight on the water. Especially the Mississippi. They needed a new plan, and quick. Marlise wasn't going to like his decision, but it was his job to keep her safe. He'd already failed once, and the next time might be the last.

Think, Cal.

He scanned the property again, and then he saw it. Salvation. He put his bird call to his lips and blew.

Chapter Three

They hit a boulder and caught a little air before settling back onto the trail. Marlise gripped the door handle on the old door as they tore across the tundra. The Jeep turned off-road vehicle had been a lifesaver when Cal found it hidden under a tarp at the back of the property. It might be the only thing that kept them out of sight long enough to find safety.

A shiver ran through her as she remembered the gunfight a few hours ago. There was no question in her mind that The Miss was doing business again. The bullets told her The Miss was worried that what Marlise knew would put her newborn business at risk. Marlise did have a secret, but she was afraid to tell Cal or Mina the truth. If they knew what she was hiding, they might kick her back to the streets, where she wouldn't last a day.

Did that make her a bad person? She was holding out on the people trying to help her, which was wrong, but she didn't think it made her a bad person. It made her a person with no good options. Telling them the truth wouldn't help matters if she couldn't cough up the proof.

"How much further?" she asked, noticing the sun was starting to set. Her back was sore from riding in the bumpy Jeep for the last two hours, and she needed to stretch her legs.

"Not much since we're almost out of gas," he said, his jaw pulsing as he avoided another rock in the nick of time. "We don't dare stop for a fill either. We're too memorable in these vests, and we can't risk taking them off. Check for a message from Mack again, please."

Marlise fished the secure phone out of her pocket and flipped it open. The last message had come through about two hours ago from Roman that they were safe and awaiting further instructions.

"He sent a message fifty minutes ago. It says 'Trigger Lake. Mack. Seven. End.' What does that mean?"

"It means Mack will extract us if we get to Trigger Lake by seven tonight. Otherwise, we're on our own."

Marlise glanced at the clock on the phone. It was a little after five. "How far is Trigger Lake?"

"An hour."

"Then we have time," she said, buoyed by the idea of getting out of this alive, even if it was only a reprieve while they regrouped.

"An hour by vehicle. We maybe have fifteen minutes before we run out of gas."

"Then we find another car. We need the servers

at Secure One to find The Miss," she said, a tremor in her words. "She knows where I am, Cal."

"We don't know that," he said, glancing at her for a moment. "She knew where we were going to be. That doesn't mean she knows where we're going."

With a deep breath in and out, Marlise tried not to let the panic take hold. "If that's the case, we need to find her before she finds us."

"Now there's something we both agree on, Mary," he said with a smile.

"Why do you call me Mary?" she asked, her words soft against the grumbling of the Jeep's motor.

He gave her a shrug. She figured he was going for nonchalant, but it didn't look that way to her. The shrug told her the answer wasn't simple. "I like the name Mary."

"But I go by Marlise now, Cal."

"Is that by choice though?" he asked, steering around another boulder on the path.

The Jeep was silent other than the growling of the engine. It was the first time she'd thought about it. Was she using Marlise by choice now or by habit? It was easy to give up Mary to become Marlise when The Madame recruited her. It was a second chance for her—a new beginning. A season of change to be someone other than Mary Liberman—a homeless nobody. Then along came The Madame who made her Marlise—a woman people depended on every day.

"Do you know what the name Mary means?" Cal asked.

"No, Cal. I grew up in foster care, trying to avoid the abuse at the hands of older kids and foster dads. There was little time to look up the meaning of my name."

When she turned to look at him, his jaw was pulsing as though he were working hard not to say something to upset her. She got it. Foster life was miserable for her, but it had been fantastic for his family. Roman was his foster brother, and they'd grown up together and fought together in the service. There were two sides to every coin. She was just one of the unlucky ones who got tails instead of heads.

"The name means rebellious. I have never known a Mary who wasn't rebellious. You included."

"I'm not rebellious. I'm lost, Cal. Lost in this big world without an identity that I can relate to."

"We're all a little bit lost, Mary. You might as well accept that now. You have several identities, but only you can decide which one you connect to the most."

"What identity do you connect to?" she asked, watching as the gas gauge hit the last line on the dial.

"I'm a ghost, Mary."

Her amused snort could be heard over the engine's sputtering as it tried to keep going despite its lack of energy. "You might be a ghost when you're on missions, but people know that Cal Newfellow runs Secure One. No one outside of Secure One knows Marlise or Mary even exists."

"That's not true. The Miss knows, and as evidenced by this day, you mean something to her. You mean something to me, Roman, Mina, Selina and Mack. We will give you your identity back and a real second chance."

The Jeep sputtered and died, coasting down the path until the last of its forward momentum was spent. "I guess that's that," Marlise muttered, grabbing her backpack off the Jeep's floor. "We better hoof it if we're going to make Trigger Lake in under two hours."

Cal turned and touched her forearm before she could get out of the car. Her yelp was immediate, and he lifted his hand from her arm as though it had burned him. When he saw the blood covering his palm, a look crossed his face that she couldn't define.

"Are you hurt?"

"It's nothing," she insisted, bringing her left arm to her side to hide it.

"You're bleeding, so it's most definitely something." He gently pulled her arm back over where he could see it. He turned his headlamp on and grabbed scissors from his bag, slicing her coat open. "Why didn't you tell me you'd been cut?"

"I don't know what happened to it," she muttered, keeping her eyes off the wound. It had been burning for hours, but she refused to let it slow her down. "It started burning in the SUV while we were under fire. It doesn't matter. We can worry about it later. We have to get to the extraction point."

With a grunt, he dug in his pack and came out with gauze and tape. Cal wrapped the arm tightly to stem the oozing blood. At first, it burned worse, but then it slowly became numb.

"I can't believe you knew you were hurt and didn't say anything." He snatched the phone from her vest and flipped it open, typing something out in silence.

"When you're a girl like me, you learn what injuries need immediate care and what injuries can be ignored. You learn to separate yourself from the pain and keep moving. You learn that you're always in pain, and there's no sense fighting against it. Stop the bleeding, accept the pain and soldier onward. Isn't that what they teach in the military too?"

Cal tucked the phone back into her pocket and held her gaze with his steely one. "The difference is, you're not a soldier in the middle of a war."

"That's where you're wrong, Cal," she said, opening the door and stepping out of the Jeep. "I've been a soldier in one war or another for the last twenty-eight years and survived them all. Don't forget that."

HE HOVERED IN the med bay while Selina worked on Mary's arm. When he discovered her injury, he'd sent a text to Roman telling him she was hurt and they should wait at all costs for them. By the time Mack got them out of there and back to Secure One, her wound had soaked two bandage wraps. She was getting paler by the minute, so he'd taken her directly to Selina. He was supposed to meet Roman and Mina in an hour, but first, he had to be sure Mary would be okay.

"It's oozing because a piece of the seat plastic is

stuck in her arm," Selina explained from where she sat working. Rather than stand over her shoulder, he forced himself to take a step back, so he didn't crowd her.

"I think a bullet must have come through and hit the back of the seat, which sent the plastic shrapnel into my arm," Marlise said. "Look at it this way. At least it's not a bullet lodged in my arm."

"Can you get it out, or do I need to find a doctor?" Cal asked, his lack of faith making Selina roll her eyes. She had sass, that woman.

"It's fine," Marlise said from where she lay on the hospital bed with her arm stretched out. She was already getting IV fluids and antibiotics and was less pale, but he still worried about infection.

"It's not fine," he snapped, and she shrank back against the bed. Selina glanced over her shoulder at him with impatience and disgust. "I'm sorry," he said, running his hand through his hair. "She's injured and acting like it's no big deal because she's afraid to be a burden. It's not fine, and we will take care of you," he promised, walking to Mary and taking her other hand. "I didn't mean to snap."

"It's okay," she promised with a shy smile. "It was a long day, and we're all tired."

"Amen," Selina whispered as she kept working. "Can you feel this?" she asked Marlise as she poked her arm.

"No, it's numb."

"Excellent. Let's get that debris out of there, and then we'll stitch you up so you can rest."

Cal knelt in front of the bed to focus Mary's attention on him. "I need to meet with Roman and Mina. Once you're patched up, have Selina help you shower and then go to bed."

"But I have to cook—"

He put his finger to her lips to hush her. "You're not going near the kitchen until tomorrow. There are plenty of premade meals available. You need to rest, or I will have to find someone here with the same blood type to give you blood, considering how much you've lost."

Marlise glanced at Selina, who nodded and added a shrug at the end. He appreciated that she didn't undermine him even if the truth was something else. He didn't know if she needed a blood transfusion, but he knew she needed rest. They were in the calm before the storm. There was a tornado on the way, and the tingle at the back of his neck was intense. He wasn't listening this morning, but he was tonight.

"I do have a headache," she admitted with a sigh.

Cal stood and kissed her forehead, stroking the hair back off her face and running a thumb down her cheek. When her eyes widened, he yanked his hand back as though the heat of her skin had burned him.

What was he doing?

He stepped back and avoided their gazes as he backed up to the door. "I'll leave you to it. Radio if you need anything, Selina. Mary, rest. I'm serious."

She gave him a salute, and he turned on his heel sharply and strode to the control room while berating himself the whole way. He had to keep his hands and lips off that woman before things happened that he couldn't take back. Mary wouldn't be part of his life once they caught The Miss, and he planned to do that sooner rather than later. Relationships were a no-no for someone like him. They caused entanglements that dulled your senses and shifted your focus away from the job at hand.

He slammed his way into the control room like a bull in a china shop, and his trained gaze picked out the vital activity in the room. His security team was in place monitoring his clients' businesses and homes. The other two people in the room took him by surprise—his brother and Mina. "I thought I told you two to rest," he said as a greeting.

"Hello to you too, brother," Roman said, biting back a smile. "What crawled up your pants and bit you in the a—"

"How's Marlise?" Mina asked, interrupting her husband's tirade.

"She's in the med bay," Cal said, running his hand through his hair again. "She has a piece of plastic in her arm because I dropped the ball." His finger in his chest punctuated his words. "She's tired, scared and lost too much blood. That's my fault."

"No," Roman said, standing and walking over to him. "That's The Miss's fault. You got Marlise out of there alive. She has lived through much worse than plastic in her arm and a little bit of bleeding. She's tougher than both of us combined, Cal."

"But she shouldn't have to be," he said, his shoulders deflating. "We should have seen this coming."

"We did," said Mina from where she sat at the computer. "We all knew if The Miss was still in play, the trial was where she would try to pinch Marlise. I just wasn't expecting it to get so far out of hand. The FBI should have given us cover to escape, and that didn't happen."

"The FBI," Cal snorted. "That must stand for Ferociously Bad Intel."

Both Roman and Mina bit their lips to hide their grins, but he saw them and let one lift his lips. He was tired and angry, but he always enjoyed a good dig at the FBI.

"What do we know?"

"We know The Miss is in play and wants Marlise," Mina said, stating the obvious. "We don't know where she is or how to find her."

"What's the chatter from the trial?"

"It's on an indefinite hiatus while the judge determines their next steps," Mina answered. "The prosecution is arguing they can't go ahead with the case if they can't get their witnesses there safely. The defense is arguing to dismiss the witnesses and continue the trial."

Cal grunted with laughter. "Sure, just continue the trial without their biggest players. Of course, the defense would want that, but we can't allow it to happen. Do we need to remand you and Marlise into FBI custody?"

"Absolutely not," Roman said, standing to his full height and blocking his wife from view. "Mina will not step foot into that circus until we have The Miss under lock and key."

"We may not have a choice if the FBI demands it," Mina said, leaning around her husband. "But I'd like to avoid it because they're zero for two in my opinion."

Cal pointed at her. "Marlise and I both wondered if someone on the inside tipped off The Miss."

"I want to yell that's impossible, but I can't," Roman said, rubbing his hands down his face. "Anything is possible when it comes to these people. The government claims they found no evidence of anyone else involved with The Madame from the field office, but that doesn't mean there isn't someone."

"I agree," Mina said, standing and stretching her leg. "It could be someone who works as a janitor or support staff. Like if Marlise could move around the Red Rye house without being noticed, this person could do the same. We can assume she heard it on the news, but until we know what happened today with our air support, we have to assume someone on the inside is pulling strings."

"Which is why neither you nor Marlise is going into FBI custody. You won't make it a day," Roman said, his tone fierce as he reached for his wife of less than a year. "I lost you once and nearly lost my mind. I won't put you into a situation where I could lose you again."

She slipped her arm around his waist and hugged him while Cal looked on. He noted a bit of jealousy toward his brother but immediately shut it down. He couldn't risk his business or life by getting involved with someone because he was horny.

Was he horny, or was he lonely?

Cal refused to answer that question. His job was to protect everyone on the team at Secure One, not just the person in his bed. Mary's face materialized, and he forced it away. He might want her in his bed, but she never would be.

"I agree," Cal said, his voice a little rougher than he expected. "Our priority is to find this woman and expose her. Once we do that, we can uncover any moles left in the FBI."

"I wish we had a place to start," Mina said, kissing Roman before returning to her computer. She stared at the screen for a moment and then started typing.

"What are you doing?" Cal and Roman asked in unison.

"Making a list of the mayors and city managers in small towns around Red Rye and Santa Macko."

"Why?" Cal asked, walking over to stand by her.

"She's looking for someone with an unusually cushy campaign fund," Roman said, a grin on his lips. "That's my girl."

Mina pointed at him, barely missing a beat on the keyboard. "If The Miss learned her lesson from The

Madame, she would need to clean the money coming in. She'll likely fall back on the same way they did it in Red Rye."

"Fair point," Cal agreed, "but that's like a needle in a haystack."

"Not untrue, but we have to start somewhere," she said, her fingers typing almost independently of her brain.

Mina's skills were why he'd hired her on at Secure One. She'd saved a client several times from being hacked by immediately shutting the hacker down and closing the door they got through. Before the trial, she was going through all of his clients' servers, looking for weaknesses. He wanted her to get back to that job, which meant they had to find The Miss sooner rather than later.

"Boss," Eric called from his booth that held the surveillance equipment for the property. "We've got company."

Cal, Roman and Mina were standing next to Eric within a second, and he pointed at the camera that ran along the fence line.

"Lock it down," Cal told the man, then turned to Mina. "Get Marlise in the bunker." He had barely finished the sentence, and she was out the door. He turned to his brother. "Shall we go meet our guests?"

Roman raised a brow and then nodded, a grim smile on his face as he reached for his gun.

Chapter Four

The bunker was silent other than Mina's grunt as she closed the door and locked it from below. When Cal first told Marlise about the bunker, she expected a doomsday scenario with cots lined up along the wall, dried food at the ready and a cache of weapons. Instead, it was filled with state-of-the-art computer and surveillance equipment, a kitchenette and bunks. Not everyone had access to the bunker either. There was a hatch in Cal's room on one end of the lodge and a hatch in the guest room at the other end of the lodge. There was also an exit from the back of the bunker that came out at the boathouse on the lake, but Cal told her if they ever took that exit, they'd better never plan on coming back.

She bit her lip, worry filling her at the thought of Cal being out there somewhere trying to keep her safe. He was one of those guys who kept his thoughts and emotions close to his vest. He was gruff and bossy, but he always had the well-being of everyone on the compound at the forefront of his mind.

Especially so since she came to work here, at least according to Roman.

"Would you like something to drink?" Mina asked, breaking into her thoughts.

Marlise shook her head no rather than answer.

"It's going to be okay," Mina promised, walking over to hug her. Since she'd gotten a new high-end prosthesis, you could barely tell that she was an amputee, but Marlise still felt guilty. The Miss had been torturing Mina while she was running from the house without thought of saving her friend.

That wasn't entirely true. She'd wanted to help Mina, but she knew if she'd gone up those stairs, she'd never have come back down. It had been wiser to get to her secret stash, or so she'd thought. Karma must have been why she hadn't made it out of the fire unscathed either. When Roman had gotten to the house, he'd found her by the front door nearly dead. He'd saved her, but not before the flames destroyed the skin on the left side of her body. It had been almost two years, but she still dealt with pain and nerve damage from the fire.

Her face was no longer symmetrical, and she couldn't smile or blink her eye well on the left side. Self-conscious, she always kept her hair over the weblike skin and wore long-sleeved shirts to hide the burns on her arm and side. Tonight, her arm was sore and tight where Selina had stitched it. The numbing medication was starting to wear off, and it felt like she'd been shot, even if it had only been plastic that had pierced her skin. Her nerves were so damaged on that arm that she worried this injury would only worsen it, but there was nothing she could do about it now.

"What's going on, Mina?" Marlise asked as she perched on the edge of a chair. "The lights went out, and Cal said that only happens if someone tries to infiltrate the perimeter."

"Someone did, but we were prepared for them this time. All of our alarms worked and alerted us to them early. Eric was sitting right at the computer when they showed up on our cameras. I don't know what's going on. Cal asked me to bring you down here, and I took off."

"Should we be worried?"

Mina shook her head with a smile. "Not even a little bit. We had so much warning that the team was on it right away. They just want to make sure we're safe until they send the all clear."

"Do you think it's The Miss?" Marlise asked, her voice wavering slightly.

Her friend's face didn't give away what she thought, but her shrug wasn't relaxed. The Miss was the reason Mina was an amputee, and the idea she had found them didn't sit well with either of them.

"No way to know. It could be anyone. Let's face it. Cal has made a few enemies himself over the years."

An eye roll slipped out, and Marlise huffed. "Sure, and it must be a coincidence that his enemies decided to break into Secure One the same night we were nearly killed going to The Madame's trial. I might look stupid, Mina, but I'm not."

"I never said you were stupid," she clarified. "I meant that we shouldn't speculate until we hear from Cal or Roman."

Mina started tapping away on a keyboard, and while Marlise had no idea what she was doing, she didn't bother asking. She wouldn't understand anyway. Mina's job was far too technical for Marlise to understand when her skills ended at how to do a basic internet search. She paced the length of the bunker, wishing she knew what was going on and if Cal and Roman were safe.

If The Miss showed up with enough people to overrun Secure One, there was no telling how long Marlise would be alive. Mina was confident Cal had found all the weak points at Secure One, but he'd said that when he was tasked with keeping her safe two years ago too.

"Stop worrying," Mina said firmly. "No one is going to get to you here. Cal won't allow it."

The scar on Marlise's arm burned to remind her what happened the last time The Madame got to her. "That's what they said before you were taken."

Mina held up a finger. "And Cal learned a hard and fast lesson about his vulnerabilities. Since Roman and I started working here, they've analyzed every angle of this property, retraced the steps The Madame's men took to get to me and turned Secure One into a fortress. Cal spared no expense in fortifying the perimeter, buying new equipment and training his men. No one walks onto this property unannounced now. That's why we're down here. Someone tried and set off every alarm in the control room."

Mina turned her attention back to the computer while Marlise started pacing again. Something big was going on above their heads, and she had a feeling she was smack-dab in the middle of it.

THE DAY CAL feared had arrived, and he had to force his mind to be calm. He didn't want to do something to put Marlise at risk again. He was already exhausted from their day on the run, but this turn of events most certainly had to do with Marlise. The then meek woman had sent him into a protective tailspin the moment he met her, and that hadn't changed. He refocused his attention on the shores of the lake rather than the woman hiding in the bunker. Tonight might be his chance to end The Miss's reign of terror.

From where they crouched in the grass, he held up one finger and flicked it to the right side.

"Only one guy?" Roman whispered. "Where are the other three we saw on the fence camera?"

"Maybe they just sent one scout to save time," Cal whispered. He scanned the area again and froze, dragging his head back to the left. "Wait. It might be a girl scout."

"A woman?"

"She just turned sideways, and it looks like it, but I can't be sure. She's one of the targets we saw on the fence camera. Wait." He paused and felt Roman tense next to him. "She just leaned her rifle down on a log and walked away."

"Walked away? It could be a trick," Roman said between clenched teeth. "We need to stop her before she gets much further. No one will get near my wife again."

"There has to be more than one scout, right? This has to be a distraction. Mack and Eric," Cal whispered into his wire, "there's only one scout. It could be a woman."

"Woman?" Mack asked in confusion.

"I can't be sure, but I don't trust this. Work your way back to the front of the lodge and cover it, then await further instructions. Roman and I will handle this girl scout."

"This doesn't feel right," Mack said.

"Agreed," Cal whispered.

"You know if we capture her, we have to turn her over to the FBI," Roman whispered.

Cal bit back the snort that tried to come out. "That depends on who she is and what she wants."

"She's got a gun that could put down a horse, and she's dressed in tactical gear with a vest. I think I know what she wants."

"What do you say we find out?" Cal asked his brother with a cock of his brow. "If she crosses the electric fence, she will need to recover from the voltage before she can speak."

The electric fences were designed to stop someone long enough for his team to secure them without scrambling too many brain cells. That didn't mean it didn't hurt, and Cal took a little joy in someone getting what they deserved when trespassing. He'd even started suggesting the fences to his security clients since they offered a level of protection even guards couldn't. A fence never had to sleep.

Cal and Roman worked their way to the right under the cover of darkness and trees. If The Miss found them, she wouldn't send one woman to Secure One. She'd send a dozen. Something was off. They paused in the woods, and they took in the tiny woman standing on the sand, spinning in a slow circle. She wore all black and had a flak jacket and combat vest, but she'd left the gun fifty yards away as though she'd forgotten it.

Cal glanced at Roman, who was crouched next to him. "It's like she's dazed or confused, not to mention her size. She's smaller than Marlise and Mina."

Roman nodded. "It's like she's a lost kid looking for her parents. The rifle is no longer a threat, but she could have a smaller pistol."

"Agreed, so watch yourself, brother. When she turns around again, we go. All we need to do is secure her arms. Let's try to avoid injuring her. I want to get some answers."

Cal moved the night vision glasses to the top of his head, and they waited inside the tree line for the woman to turn away. When she did, they seized the opportunity.

"Lights, lights, lights!" Cal yelled into his wire as they ran out of the trees.

Awash in light, they watched the woman fall to her knees with her hands up. "I surrender! I surrender!" she yelled.

Roman and Cal glanced at each other, but slowed their approach, watching for any tricks. They both had dead aim on the trembling woman still on her knees. Hell, she looked like a kid from what Cal could see. Her blond hair spilled out from under her black stocking cap, and her petite frame was nearly swallowed up by the tactical vest.

Looks can be deceiving, a voice whispered.

Didn't Cal know that better than anyone? He didn't need a reminder. "What do you want?" he asked, only a few feet away from her now.

"I want to surrender," she whimpered. "I surrender."

"Lay down on your stomach and put your hands behind your back," Roman ordered as he glanced at Cal.

She did as he instructed, even crossing her ankles and lifting them to be secured. Roman nodded at him, so Cal holstered his gun and motioned for Roman to cover him while he zip-tied the woman's hands together. He left her feet unsecured so she could walk.

"I'm going to ask you again. What do you want?" Cal said, walking around in front of the girl. She was young, and her face told of the horrors she'd lived.

He'd seen that haunted look in another woman's eyes before. She was currently hiding out in his bunker.

"I don't want to do this anymore. I need help. Please, help me."

The girl started crying softly, and Cal glanced up at Roman, who gave him the what-the-heck hands. Cal shrugged and grabbed hold of the woman's arm, helping her up. "Consider yourself surrendered. Where are your friends? There were four of you."

"They left," she said through her tears, and Cal lowered a brow at her. "I swear. I'm alone."

"Come on," Roman said, grabbing her other arm. "The fences will get them if she's lying. We need answers from her before the other three arrive with backup."

Cal sighed, but agreed with his brother. "This isn't a trick?" he asked the woman, who shook her head as tears streamed down her face.

"I'm tired, hungry and scared," she whispered. "I just want this to be over."

Cal released her arm, jogged over and grabbed her rifle. He covered their backs on their way to the lodge just in case others were lurking. Why did this woman think she had to surrender? Was she being forced to do something against her will? She was part of the group that had arrived near the fence, but where did her companions go? Even if the other three still wandered the property, they didn't have the firepower or the skills to outgun or outrun his men—none of this made sense.

Her head hung lower and lower until her chin touched her chest, and her feet shuffled along as though they weighed one thousand pounds. It wasn't from dread or a ploy to hold them up. It was pure exhaustion. He had two secret weapons he could deploy to get to the bottom of this.

Mina and Marlise.

Cal's mind went straight to Marlise, the woman he'd rescued with his plane two years ago, who'd worn the same look of fear and exhaustion. Maybe she could be the one to get answers from this woman. If they got lucky, Mina might be able to tag her as one of The Madame's, and they'd be one step closer to bringing The Miss down. Cal had promised Marlise last summer he wouldn't stop until she was behind bars, but that was easier said than done. Regardless of how often Cal put his ear to the ground, it was radio silence.

The woman he'd been protecting for over a year now deserved to be free. She had seen things in life that no one should, but she still got up every day and tried to make a difference at Secure One. Cal wanted Marlise to be free to find happiness. She hadn't known a lot of happy times in her life. Raised in foster care and then put out on the streets at eighteen, she had seen things no one should have to see. By twenty-four, she was running the household of a madwoman hell-bent on destroying other women's lives. By twenty-seven, she was recovering from burns over a quarter of her body and wondering why she was fighting to live.

Cal wanted—no, he needed—to be the one to give her that answer. He was confident the woman before them was the key to unlocking The Miss's secrets. He was less confident that doing that wouldn't result in carnage they wouldn't see coming.

Chapter Five

"Who is she?" Mina asked when she joined them in the control room.

"We're hoping you can tell us," Cal answered.

"You're sure she was alone?"

"From what we can tell," Roman said from where he leaned on a table. "We know she wasn't alone when they tripped the alarms in the woods. When we hauled her in off the lakeshore she told us the other women had left."

"That doesn't make any sense," Mina said, biting her lip for a moment. "Do you think she's a decoy?"

"All I know is, this entire compound is lit up like it's daytime, and guards are at battle stations. If someone approaches, we'll see them coming. We need to talk to this woman and find out who she is and what she wants. She kept saying 'I surrender' until she broke down into tears." Cal lifted his palms up to relay his confusion.

"She also said she was tired, hungry, scared and wanted help," Roman added.

"She didn't put up a fight?" Mina asked with surprise.

Roman walked over to his wife. "No. It was like she wanted to get caught. She even walked away from her gun, which is suspicious, if you ask me."

"Let's see her."

Cal hit a button on the computer, and the two-way mirror activated. A woman sat alone at a table, huddled in a chair with her arms wrapped around her knees. She'd been checked for explosives and bugs and wore nothing but gray sweats, with her blond hair pulled back in a ponytail. She reminded Cal so much of Marlise in the early days—scared and alone.

"That's Charlotte."

"You recognize her?" Roman asked with surprise.

"Yes! She's from the house in Red Rye. She was one of The Miss's drug mules, but was just being introduced to it when everything went down."

"She's higher up in The Miss's organization?" Cal asked.

"I can't say," Mina said with a shake of her head. "I don't know what's gone on over the last two years. Something has because that's not the same woman I knew."

"What do you mean?" Cal asked as Mina stepped up to the mirror.

"She's lost weight. Easily fifty pounds. She looks sickly and terrified."

"Maybe she's hooked on the drugs The Miss was

making her traffic?" Roman asked. "Could be that's how she was being convinced to stay."

"That's possible, but she doesn't appear to be tweaking. She just looks…"

"Tired, sad and scared," Cal finished. "She looks like Marlise did when we first picked her up."

Mina pointed at him. "Exactly."

"We need information from her," Roman said, putting his arm around his wife. "Are you willing to ask the questions? She's not restrained, but I don't think she's a threat."

"She never was," Mina agreed. "She was always just scared and confused in Red Rye. In her current condition, I could take her even without my prosthesis. Something isn't right here," she said on a hum. "Charlotte was only one step above Marlise in how she interacted with the men on dates. She could talk to them with more confidence, but she was scared. The Miss sent her on dates with older men because they demanded less of her."

"She didn't want to be part of the house either?" Cal asked.

"Absolutely not. She was tricked into it just like Marlise. A few days before the fire, she secretly told me she was scared and showed me several hand-shaped bruises on her thighs."

A word dropped from Roman's lips that summed up exactly how everyone felt about what went on in Red Rye, Kansas. "Do you think this is a defection then?"

"Honestly, from what I see right now, yes, but I don't trust The Miss."

"Do you think Charlotte will talk to you?" Cal asked, nervously tapping the floor with his boot. "We need to know why she's here, and we need to know fast."

"I could go in and talk to her, but if I were you, I'd send in Marlise."

"Absolutely not," Cal said immediately. "Marlise is not getting near this woman."

Roman lifted a brow at Cal, but he didn't care. Marlise had gone through enough because of The Miss and was finally putting things right in her head. He wouldn't throw her back into that life when other people could ask the questions.

"I'll go in with her," Mina quickly said, "but Charlotte will see me for what I am. An FBI agent. She'll connect with Marlise as someone who lived through the same things she did."

"She's right," Roman said, his brow still in the air.

"Marlise is just getting back on an even keel almost two years later, and you want to stick her in there and bring it all back? No. I won't allow it."

Mina gently touched his arm until he made eye contact with her. "Don't you think we should let Marlise decide? She's a grown woman and a lot stronger than you give her credit for now. If I go in there alone, I could do more harm than good. Marlise has earned the right to make her own choice about this."

Cal ground his teeth together to keep the scathing rebuttal from escaping. The last thing he wanted to do was expose Marlise to anything that had to do with The Miss, but he also knew Mina might be right. Marlise had a gentle touch with even the toughest of his men. She'd hand them a cookie, and they'd be putty in her hands.

"Fine, but she's never alone with her."

Mina and Roman both nodded in agreement.

"I'll go talk to Marlise. Mina, would you grab some food from the kitchen? If she's going in, I want her armed."

Mina grinned. "Meet back here in ten."

MARLISE HATED BEING cut off from whatever was going on, but she had followed Mina's orders to stay in her room. She trusted that Cal would fill her in soon, but that didn't keep her from pacing the small space while she waited.

Her room was right next door to Cal's. In fact, when she moved to Secure One last summer, he'd installed adjoining room doors, so she had access to the bunker at all times. A smile tipped her lips up when she remembered the argument they'd had about where she'd be living. She had insisted a cabin by the lake would be fine, but Cal had flat-out refused to hear of it. He was adamant that it wasn't safe for her to be anywhere she didn't have instant access to the bunker. If tonight were any indication, maybe he'd been right.

A knock on the door made Marlise jump. "Mary? It's Cal. We need to talk."

Her shoulders relaxed as she walked to the door and checked the peephole to make sure Cal was alone before she opened it. The door was no sooner open than he was in the room and it was closed again.

Cal was…formidable. You wouldn't want to meet him in a dark alley if you operated on the wrong side of the law. He wore full sleeves of beautiful tattoos featuring the Greek gods that she'd spent hours gazing at without him even knowing. She'd memorized their placement, colorings and little nuances of shadows and light. Marlise suspected he had more, but she was far too drawn to him to ask where and if she could see them. She needed to stay ten feet away from Cal at all times.

"What's going on?" she asked, taking a step back to remind herself not to touch him. "And don't lie to me."

"I wouldn't do that, Mary, but there has been a development."

"The Miss."

He tipped his head in agreement. "It appears so. We took a woman into custody, and Mina made an identification."

"You captured The Miss?" Marlise stumbled backward and would have fallen if Cal hadn't grabbed her.

"Are you okay?" he asked, and she nodded robotically, even though the heat of his hand seared her arm.

"I'm f-fine. I wasn't expecting you to say you had The Miss."

"We don't," he said patiently. "Mina identified the woman we took into custody as Charlotte. Do you remember her?"

Marlise nodded again, but couldn't make words leave her mouth. *Why is Charlotte here?*

"There were originally three other women with her, but she was alone by the time we took her into custody."

"Where are the other three?" Marlise asked, her voice low and shaky.

"That's what we need to find out. Mina thinks you're the best person to talk to Charlotte. Were you friends with her in Red Rye?"

The nod she gave him was exact. "If you can call what went on in that house friendly. Charlotte was a lot like me. She didn't like the men, but she couldn't find a way to ingratiate herself to The Miss the way I did. She was just starting as a drug mule when the fire happened."

"How did she feel about that? Did she talk to you about it?"

Marlise wrapped her arms around her waist and swallowed over her dry throat. "She had only been doing it about a month, but she didn't like it. She begged The Miss to book her with the older men. She said they didn't expect her to do as much."

Cal's nod was sharp, but his smile was comforting. "That's exactly what Mina said."

"Was that a test?" Marlise asked with confusion. "I wouldn't lie to you, Cal." She turned her back and walked over to her bed, putting distance between them so she could think. If Charlotte was here alone, it was either a trap or something terrible had happened, which meant she was sick or hurt.

"I wasn't testing you, Mary. I was gathering information. Mina may have been told one thing while you were privy to something else."

Her shoulders rolled inward, and she dropped her chin to her chest. "Is Charlotte hurt?"

"Not that we're aware of. Why?"

"It doesn't make sense that she's here, Cal." She stood to pace the room again. "Why would she think she could just walk in and surrender? It has to be a trap."

"It could be. That's why we need to talk to Charlotte."

Marlise squared her shoulders and nodded. "Take me to her."

Cal stepped up into her space, and she fought against taking a step back. His gaze was intense as he drank her in, but she wouldn't back down. His brown eyes darkened to deep chocolate before he spoke. "You don't have to do this. You're just starting to find level ground, and I don't like reminding you of your time in Red Rye under The Miss's rule."

"I'm reminded every time I look in the mirror, Cal," she said, stiffening her spine to appear taller. "I'm not the fragile flower you think I am. I've gone through a lot in this life. Things I haven't told anyone. Talking to Charlotte will be the least difficult thing I've done in my life."

He took another step before he grasped her shoulders, connecting them in a way she couldn't deny. "I don't think you're a fragile flower. You're stronger than I'll ever be, and I'm twice your size. The last thing I want to do is cause you pain though."

"You need answers, right?" she asked, and he nodded, his jaw pulsing as though he hated to admit it. "Then let's go get them."

MINA HANDED MARLISE a plate with a sandwich, cookies and a glass of milk. "Your job at the house in Red Rye was to take care of the girls. Let's go at it from that angle."

She opened the door, and Marlise walked through, the moment captured in Cal's eye as he stood in the recording booth looking through the two-way mirror. He had a wire on both women, so they could hear loud and clear what was said in the room. Roman stood beside him while Mack stood outside the room the women were in, just in case muscle was needed. Cal didn't think it would be. It was easy to see Charlotte wasn't a threat to anyone except possibly The Miss.

"Charlotte," Marlise said to the woman sitting at the table. "I can't believe it's you!" She set the plate and glass down on the table and pulled her into a hug.

His girl could act. He had to give her that.

No. She's not your girl, Cal. You don't deserve a girl. Your lifestyle doesn't lend itself to having any vulnerability in your life.

"Marlise!" Charlotte exclaimed. "You're safe!"

"Yes," Marlise answered, pushing the food toward the woman before she sat down. "I'm the head chef here now. Mina got me the job." She hooked a thumb at Mina, who had sat down at the table.

"Agent August, you mean?" Charlotte asked quite suspiciously.

"Not anymore," Mina clarified. "I left the FBI after what happened in Red Rye. I want to help people, Charlotte, not hurt them. After The Madame was caught, I spent a year helping the FBI take care of the girls from other houses."

Charlotte looked to Marlise, who nodded. "It's true. She helped many girls just like us get therapy and find jobs."

"She didn't help me."

"We couldn't find you, or she would have," Marlise clarified. "Where have you been for two years?"

Charlotte refused to answer. She picked up the sandwich, took a bite and washed it down with a swallow of milk. It was like she hadn't eaten in days, and she attacked the food without another word while Mina and Marlise stared at each other.

"She's starving," Roman said while the woman moaned as she ate.

"I haven't eaten real food in days," Charlotte whispered when she finished the milk. "I don't even care if that was drugged. It was so good."

Mina leaned forward across the table. "The food wasn't drugged, Charlotte. We would never do that to you. We don't know why you're here, but you must be desperate, so why don't you talk to us?"

"How did you get here tonight, Charlotte?" Marlise gently asked.

"We had a car with a preprogrammed GPS to this location."

"We?"

Charlotte nodded and leaned back in her chair, wrapping her arms around her waist. "There were four of us."

"We noticed that on our cameras," Mina said. "But you were the only one who came in via the lake."

"We were just supposed to scout the property and find a way to attack. As soon as we saw the electric fences, we knew that her plan wouldn't work."

"Her?" Marlise asked.

"The Miss," Charlotte whispered after she swallowed nervously. "She wants you. She said you know too much and can't be allowed to testify at the trial. The Madame's men were supposed to have killed you both two years ago, but they failed."

"Why did she wait so long to come after Marlise?" Mina asked with heavy suspicion.

"I don't know," Charlotte answered, and Cal believed her.

"This girl followed orders, but she wasn't privy to

important information," Cal said, and Roman nodded his agreement. "She's also terrified. You can see it in her demeanor."

"She reminds me of Marlise when we first talked to her after the fire—skittish and on guard."

Cal didn't say that Marlise was still skittish and on guard, but she'd earned the right to be. Her life had been hell, and trusting people would never be easy. She trusted him though. She'd told him as much several times over the last year. At least she trusted him with her safety. She shouldn't trust him with her heart or her body.

He shook his head and focused on the women in the room again. He had no right to her heart or her body. He was a loner. A ghost. Someone with no roots. He had to remember that before he did something to jeopardize both his life and Marlise's.

Chapter Six

It was easy to see that the woman sitting across from her wasn't the same woman Marlise had lived with two years ago. What wasn't easy to see was why. She knew Cal must be getting frustrated in the control booth with their lack of answers, but she couldn't push Charlotte to open up to them until she believed they'd help her. That was life experience speaking. Marlise remembered those first days and weeks after the fire at Red Rye when she was scared and in pain. She hated that Charlotte was feeling the same way now.

"You've been with The Miss this whole time?" Mina asked.

Marlise forced herself not to grimace. She would have approached the question with a gentler tone, but Mina was the one trained in interrogation.

Charlotte was silent for several seconds before she nodded. "I don't want to live that way anymore." Tears fell down her cheeks, and Marlise handed her a tissue. She dabbed at her face and then twisted the tissue in her hand.

"Where are the other girls you were with tonight?"

"Gone. They said trying to access the property by the lake was a waste of time, and it wouldn't work."

"It is, and it wouldn't," Mina said with conviction. "You had already tripped the alarms on every part of the property."

Charlotte lifted her chin, even if it was still trembling. "I wanted to get caught. When no one came out after we tromped around in the woods, I convinced them to let me check out the lake alone. They said it was my funeral and they were leaving. I told them I'd meet up with them at the car."

"Do you know where the car is?" Mina asked, glancing toward the mirror.

"Long gone," Charlotte answered. "I gave them a head start back to the car before leaving the woods along the lake. I wanted to miss our agreed-upon time so they'd know I wasn't coming and take off. They don't care. I'm expendable."

"Weren't you afraid of getting shot?" Marlise asked. "You had to know someone would be waiting for you once you showed yourself."

Charlotte nodded, and a tear ran down her cheek. Marlise's heart squeezed tightly in her chest. She remembered what it was like to live that life and how terrifying it was.

"I knew it was a possibility, but I hoped I'd be okay if I surrendered right away. It was a chance I was willing to take. We're never far from death when used as pawns in other people's games. At least I had the control this time."

Mina and Marlise both nodded, but they glanced at each other. Marlise saw the nervousness in Mina's eyes and was sure it reflected in her own. They didn't know if Charlotte was telling the truth or if she was trying to give the other group time to penetrate the perimeter with more firepower. Marlise had to believe that wasn't the case.

"Why did you think it was safe to come here?" Marlise asked the question burning in everyone's mind.

"You're free of The Madame, right?"

Marlise made a so-so gesture with her hand. "I get paid to work here, and I'm not being forced to stay, but I also can't leave as long as The Miss is out there."

Charlotte's shoulder shrugged in a motion of weighted fatigue. "That's true, but you know you're protected here, and no one makes you do…" She paused and closed her eyes on an inhaled breath. "Things you don't want to do with men, right?"

Mina took the girl's trembling hand, nodding at Marlise to answer. "That's right. I don't have to do anything I don't want to do."

Her eyes came open, and she stared into Marlise's with round, blue, hopeful ones. "Then, the way I saw it, this was a safe place. I know I'll go to jail eventually, but I had to get away from The Miss," she whispered, tears streaming down her face. "She's making us do bad things. Worse things than we already do. She wants us to kill people!"

Charlotte broke down into uncontrollable sobbing, and Mina stood, making the cut motion at her neck before trying to comfort Charlotte. Marlise sat back against the chair and tried to process what the woman had told them, but she didn't know where to start.

"Marlise," Mina said sharply, dragging her attention back to the room. "We need to get her to the med bay."

Mina hadn't finished her sentence before Mack opened the door, rushed in and caught Charlotte just as she passed out. He was running with her down the hallway to the med bay before either of the women could speak.

"Life just got interesting," Mina said, staring at the empty chair at the table.

"Again," Marlise finished.

"THE PLOT THICKENS," Cal said once they gathered together again. Charlotte was in the med bay with Selina, being hydrated with an IV and something to calm her. "I'm not sure what happened in there to have her react that way."

"I am," Marlise said from the corner where she leaned against the wall. She walked over to them and leaned on the table. "I remember the plunge of adrenaline when I realized I was safe here. That's what happened. Charlotte realized she was safe."

"You believed her then?" Cal asked, walking over and standing next to her.

"Does it make me naive if I say yes?" she asked, glancing at him and then Mina.

"No," Mina said. "I feel the same way. I just wish we had gotten more out of her before she collapsed. I have so many questions."

"We all do," Mack said. He'd been standing at attention at the door as though he were a sentry for the people inside. In a way, Mack was, but he was so much more than that. He was a brother in arms, and when he needed a place to recover from the trauma he'd suffered in the military, Cal was able to offer him a place to heal and, eventually, a place to work and find a community again.

"Let's make a list of questions, so when she's able, we can ask them," Roman said, pulling out a chair and sitting at the sprawling table in the conference room. Everyone sat except for Cal, who wrote the questions on a whiteboard as they were asked.

Cal stood at the board and pointed at each question. "Here's what I know. We have two major questions we need answered. The first—is The Miss working alone or at the direction of The Madame? The second—where is The Miss hiding out, and how do we get to her?"

"Followed by, is it only The Miss from Red Rye behind this, or did the few who scattered during the raids link up?" Roman finished.

"How many of the misses were unaccounted for after the raids?" Cal asked Mina.

"There were twelve houses, and four didn't have a miss. At least no one fessed up to it."

"Wouldn't the other women have singled her out?" Cal asked, but Mina shook her head.

"Absolutely not. They were traumatized and scared of their shadows. There's no way they would risk their life by ratting out their miss."

"I agree," Marlise said with a nod. "I wouldn't have if you'd caught her that day."

"But then she could start another house and do this to more women. Wouldn't you do anything within your power to stop that?" Cal asked, his head tipped to the side in confusion.

Marlise crossed her arms over her chest and held his gaze. She wasn't backing down on her statement. "You're a man who doesn't know the first thing about being tricked, used and abused, Cal Newfellow. You can stand up there and be judgy and righteous because you've never been sold like a piece of property and treated like garbage. Until you have been, never suggest anything I do is wrong."

Mina stood and put her arm around Marlise, squeezing her. "It's okay. I don't think he meant to be judgy or righteous."

Cal walked around the table and approached her. "I'm sorry. You're right. I can't make a blanket statement like that if I haven't been in the situation. I apologize for being disrespectful. That was never my intention. I was simply trying to suss out the major players here."

Marlise swallowed around the dryness in her throat that being near him always caused. If only he knew how he affected her, but she was glad he didn't. She was glad he didn't know how attracted she was to him. Besides, it was probably nothing more than reverse Stockholm syndrome now that she was here and he was the one protecting her.

A little voice inside her head laughed. *Sure. Keep telling yourself that.*

"I shouldn't have said that. I'm sorry." She broke eye contact and looked away, ashamed that everyone in the room saw her lose her cool.

"No," Roman said from where he sat, and she glanced up at him. "Everyone in this room has a right to their opinion and respect when it comes to anything that directly affects them. You don't have to apologize for standing up for yourself and Charlotte."

"That's what I'm worried about, see," Marlise said, glancing between everyone in the room except Cal. She could feel his gaze on her with an intensity she was afraid to confront. "Charlotte is a new defect from the house, so if someone says the wrong thing or asks the wrong question, she might get scared and clam up because she thinks we're judging her."

Marlise's shoulders slumped, and she lowered herself to a chair, completely ignoring the man standing next to her until he walked around the table again and gave her breathing room. That was the most forceful she'd been about her opinions since she'd arrived here, and now she was worried she would lose her job for crossing the one person who had hired her.

"She's right," Cal said from where he stood by the board, and Marlise snapped her head up in surprise.

"I am?"

Cal, Roman and Mack all chuckled together while Mina reached over and squeezed her hand.

"You are. I forget that I have a privilege here that you, Charlotte and Mina don't have, and that privilege is being male. I have power, strength and the ability to make my own choices. The women with The Miss don't, and I need to remember my place. This is what I think we should do, but I want you and Mina in agreement before we move forward."

"We're listening," Mina assured him, and he leaned over on the table, his size an unscalable wall against the outside world in Marlise's mind.

"I want one or the other of you with Charlotte tonight. Mack will pull guard duty when you're there, alternating with Eric." Marlise saw Mack nod out of the corner of his eye. "Once Charlotte is strong enough to answer these two big questions, I want Mary—" Cal paused and cleared his throat. "Sorry, Marlise to ask them conversationally. No Mina, Selina or Mack in the room. We will record the conversation and listen to it when you're done. Do you think she will be at ease enough then to discuss the finer points of the organization? At least so we have a starting point?"

Marlise glanced at Mina, who nodded and shrugged

one shoulder. "All I can do is try, Cal. I'll try my hardest because there are more girls like Charlotte with The Miss. If what she said is true, and The Miss is teaching them how to kill, we need to find her and stop this train before it goes off the rails."

"Everyone in this room agrees on that," Roman said. "The sooner, the better too. Mina, let's head to the control room to look at the video footage from the fence cam. Maybe you'll recognize one of the other three women in the shot. Marlise can take the first shift with Charlotte."

"Sounds good. Then I will dig into the files of the women we rescued from the four houses with the missing misses. If I find any who have disappeared again after we helped them, that's another lead we can follow if necessary."

With the plan agreed upon, everyone stood and filed out to assume their positions. Before Marlise could leave, Cal gently grasped her arm and held her in place. "I'm truly sorry, Mary. It was never my intention to insult or upset you."

"I know, Cal," she whispered with her gaze pinned to the floor. "It's fine. Consider it forgotten."

He tipped her chin up and forced her to meet his gaze. "It's not fine, and it's not forgotten. It was a lesson I learned and won't forget. You might think I believe that brute force and barked orders get things done around here, but that's not true. I listen to what my team has to say and consider everyone's opinion on the situation before going forward. That's what keeps everyone alive."

"And I'm a member of the team by default, right? I'm here because I need protection from the bad guys still after me, but as soon as you catch them, you'll cut me loose?"

"Wrong. You're a member of this team because you earned your place here. We might be closer than ever to the bad guys who are out to get you, but catching them doesn't mean you're off the team. Catching them gives you the chance to make your own decisions about your future. You're part of this team for as long as you want to be. I think we work well together, and you give the group insight into issues around jobs that we wouldn't have had without you here. Don't underestimate your contributions to this team, Mary. Understood?"

Marlise nodded rather than spoke. She was afraid her voice would hold all the emotions welling inside her chest. She felt pride that she was an integral part of a team that needed her insight as much as she needed theirs. She knew what she had to do as she walked down to the med bay to check on Charlotte. Once she had more answers, she would put her fear aside and talk to Cal. It wasn't fair to put the fight for her independence squarely on his shoulders. She would have to dig deep, trust the man who was keeping her safe and prove that she was a team player once and for all.

Chapter Seven

"How is she?" Marlise asked Mina when she walked into the med bay the following day. She'd gone to bed about 2:00 a.m. and then got up at 6:00 a.m. to make breakfast for everyone before her next shift with Charlotte. Cal was insistent she stay out of the kitchen, but he didn't understand that cooking helped her relax when things were stressful. Besides, she'd suffered worse injuries while working in Red Rye and never broke stride, so a small cut on her arm wouldn't slow her down.

"She's been sleeping most of the night. She just woke up and had some juice. She was much calmer, so we let her rest until you arrived," Mina explained, standing outside the door to the med bay.

"I brought her breakfast," Marlise said, holding up the tray. "I will let her eat and then ask the big questions. Time is short."

"Agreed," Mina said with a head nod. "Selina needed a break, so I told her you and Mack had the space covered. She's going to grab a shower and some food. That will give you the opening you need to ask your questions."

"I can do this," Marlise said, taking a deep breath. "We have to stop The Miss before she gets girls to kill for her. I don't think they'd be doing it willingly."

"Me either," Mina answered with her lips pursed. "The idea that The Miss is teaching young, innocent women to be assassins for her gain is terrifying and enraging. If the FBI doesn't stop her, we will."

Marlise glanced over her shoulder at Mack before leaning into Mina's ear. "Will we get in trouble if we don't hand Charlotte over to the authorities?"

"Turning Charlotte over to the authorities would only put her at risk, and other than trespassing, they'd have nothing to charge her with right now. She defected and essentially claimed asylum from The Miss. Besides, sex trafficked women aren't held accountable for anything they do against their will that breaks the law."

"Okay," Marlise said with a nod. "If she asked, I wanted to reassure her, and I know she'll ask."

"Good luck, and let Mack know if you need anything."

Mina waved and walked down the hallway while Marlise entered the med bay and smiled at Charlotte. "Good morning. I brought you some breakfast. I thought you might be hungry."

"Good morning, Marlise. I'm glad to see you. I was worried when I woke up and Mina was here."

"She's a friend, Charlotte," Marlise promised,

sliding the tray across the table so she could eat. "Mina doesn't work for the FBI anymore."

"That's what she said. She told me that her boss was The Madame's husband. I would never have expected an FBI agent to be married to a woman like The Madame."

"Money will corrupt people fast and ugly, Charlotte," Marlise said, pulling the chair up to sit by her friend. "We saw it over and over at the house in Red Rye. I bet you've seen it more since."

"Like The Miss," Charlotte said between bites of toast and eggs.

"She was angling to be the closest confidante of The Madame's. We saw that in Red Rye."

"Now she's decided to be the woman."

"You mean she's not working for The Madame still?" Marlise asked, hoping Cal was recording the way he promised. She hadn't expected Charlotte to start spilling the tea within seconds of sitting down, but she didn't want to stop her. At the very least, she noticed Mack move closer to the door, so he must be listening.

"How could she? The Madame is in prison."

Marlise shrugged, hoping she looked relaxed. "There are plenty of people running outside operations from behind bars. I wondered if there were plans for The Miss to continue if The Madame was caught."

"From what The Miss said, The Madame never expected to get caught. She was too confident that no one would ever tag her, so she never put any backup plans in place. Anyway, that's what I gathered from The Miss over the last two years."

"And she's not working with any of the other misses right now?"

Charlotte waved her hands in front of her chest. "Not that I'm aware of, but I didn't know the ones from the other houses. We got a lot of new girls joining the ranks though, so I can't say for sure. They didn't catch all the misses?"

"No," Marlise admitted on a breath. "There were four houses where they couldn't prove who was running them."

"And no girl would snitch her out if she valued her life."

Marlise pointed at her and hoped Cal was recording. He needed to hear that she wasn't the only one who believed that. "Exactly. It's entirely possible the misses were taken in with the other girls and then processed back out as survivors. There's no way to know for sure."

"I can tell you that no one else is as high up as our Miss. She's on the top rung and keeping everyone else at the bottom. You only get the information needed for each specific job. I usually overhear things because part of my job is cleaning and laundry duties, so I'm around her trailer more than anyone else. If we aren't doing chores, or out working a job, we're expected to be training."

"Training?"

Charlotte nodded, but dropped the toast back to the tray and pushed it away. "Working out, running, working on our combat training or practicing at the range."

"You were serious when you said she's teaching you to kill?"

"Dead serious," Charlotte said, "no pun intended. If you refuse, that's how you end up."

"Did all the other girls from Red Rye run with The Miss that night?" Marlise asked. She had the answer to one question for Cal, and now she needed to get the second one.

Her nod was enough of an answer.

Trying to gauge the size of the current operation, Marlise asked, "So, ten of you left Red Rye, including The Miss and the two guards?"

"Yes." Charlotte nodded. "But more have been added since then."

"Were you warned about the fire?"

"From what I could understand by eavesdropping on The Miss in the van, she was the one to tell The Madame that Mina was an agent. The Madame wanted Mina tortured to find out what she knew, and then killed to ensure she couldn't spill any secrets."

"But they already knew Mina was an agent. Mina's boss put her there."

Charlotte held up her hands again. "True, but The Miss didn't know that. She was livid that she'd been lied to."

"I don't have any solid memories of the timeline from that night because of the fire. What happened?"

"The Miss sent us to the airport to wait for her and the guards. By the time she joined us, everything had changed. She had changed. Suddenly, her need to please The Madame was gone, and she just barked orders and expected you to comply. She told us we were going by car so The Madame couldn't find us."

"But why? It was another year before The Madame was caught."

"She didn't know any of that though. She also didn't know The Madame put Mina in the house. She knew that an FBI agent had been living with us for a year, and that put everything she'd worked for at risk. If you want my opinion, I think she saw it as a chance to break away from The Madame and do what she'd always wanted to do."

"Run the show?" Marlise asked, and Charlotte nodded once.

"What happened after you left the airport in Red Rye? Where did you go?"

"A van showed up and we rode in it, blindfolded, for days. Breaks were always in the woods, and there were never any signs to tell us where we were. When we got to where we were going, it was hot. That's all I know."

"Hot?"

"Hot, dusty, doesn't rain much, and there are lots of cactus around the mobile homes. The new home base is in the middle of nowhere."

"You live in mobile homes?"

Charlotte's shrug was jerky. "They might be old

camping trailers? I'm not sure. They're silver on the outside."

"How many trailers are there, and does The Miss have her own?" Marlise asked, leaning in as she waited for the answer. She was getting the information Cal needed, and she didn't want to give up now. She had to get as much from Charlotte as possible before the girl got too tired.

"The Miss has a big trailer in the middle," she explained and then motioned to show how the other trailers surrounded it like sunrays.

"What happens if a girl doesn't want to stay?"

Charlotte's head shook, and her lip trembled. "Not a good idea. Not a good idea."

Before Marlise could say anything more, she broke down into racking sobs again, and Marlise took her hand to comfort her, knowing Selina would swoop in and give her something to calm her.

Mack walked in and took Charlotte's other hand with both of his, his thumbs rubbing over the back of her hand in a pattern that seemed to calm her friend. He motioned for her to go, which meant Cal wanted her.

She stood, gave the now hiccupping woman one last look and steeled herself for what was to come.

"WHAT STATES HAVE cactus besides Arizona and California?" Cal asked the team gathered around the control room and computers.

"New Mexico, California, Arizona, Texas, Nevada and Utah," Mina reeled off.

"That's a lot of acreage," Roman said.

"But we narrowed it down to six states," Cal added, his mind spinning as he tried to sort through the information Charlotte had shared. "Mina, you said that the women who went on the drug dates flew to large events. Do you remember what cities? Was there one they went to the most?"

"I don't know."

"I thought you scheduled the dates," Cal said, frustration forcing his hand into his hair, still cut in the military high and tight style.

"I did the regular dates, but the travel dates were different. I scheduled the girl out of the house on the calendar, but The Miss dealt with the rest. I called the pilot and let him know to check for a flight plan for what date, but I wasn't privy to any other information."

Marlise walked in the door, and Cal motioned her over. "Great job, Mary," he whispered, putting his arm around her and squeezing her. "That was flawless questioning."

"I wasn't questioning her," Marlise said, shrugging under his hand. "I just let her talk. Maybe once she rests, she can tell us more. I don't think she knows where they're based though. The vibe I got from her is The Miss doesn't want them to know."

"Charlotte said they were blindfolded the entire drive to the new camp. The Miss must be paranoid,"

Mina said with a head shake. "Paranoid people are dangerous when they feel trapped."

"Our next question when she's rested again is, are they always blindfolded when they leave the camp?" Cal said. "Mina, did you recognize any of the other women with Charlotte at the fence?"

"No," Mina answered. "The other three were not from Red Rye, at least the best I could tell from the grainy images."

Cal turned and took Marlise's shoulders. "Do you have a gut feeling about where they might be based now?"

He noticed Marlise glance around the room before she shook her head. "Could be anywhere. I'm from Arizona, and there are a lot of cacti there." She shrugged, but Cal could see she was filled with fear.

Cal released her and turned to the rest of the room. "I want to know how The Miss is funding this."

Mina let out a loud *ha* from her chair by the computer. "The Miss controlled the money in Red Rye. I know she was skimming. She got on the boss's good side and then ate up every detail of the operation. I was more afraid of The Miss than I was The Madame," she said with a shoulder shrug. "We never saw The Madame, but The Miss was ruthless."

"And since The Madame was never there, it would have been easy to skim money without anyone suspecting?" Cal asked.

"She's right," Marlise agreed. "The few dates I went on, I was supposed to get a certain amount of money, but sometimes I got a lot more. I gave it to The Miss and then got my cut, which wasn't much. She easily could have kept anything extra before she logged it for The Madame."

"Is it a stretch to say that she could have been running her own enterprise by piggybacking on The Madame's business?" Cal asked.

"When it comes to sex trafficking and drugs, anything is possible," Mina said with a sigh. "There was so much money coming into Red Rye, not to mention drugs, it wouldn't be hard for her to build up a parachute fairly quickly without The Madame ever knowing."

"I need to ask Charlotte how The Miss pays them," Marlise said, adding it to her list on a notepad.

"Or doesn't pay them," Roman said. "Charlotte indicated it wasn't a good idea for a girl to say no. Maybe she's just holding them hostage and forcing them to work."

"That or she's promising them great returns on the back end once their operation is up and running," Mina added. "After living with her for a year, I could see her pulling that off with those women. Maybe she's dangling part ownership in the adventure."

"Possible," Marlise agreed. "She was always spouting girl power when she wanted us to get on board with an idea."

Mina started to giggle until they were full-on laughing to the point they couldn't stop. Cal helped

Marlise to a chair, waiting while she wiped her cheeks with her shoulders.

"I'm sorry," she said with contriteness. "It probably doesn't seem like a laughing matter to you, but you'd understand if you'd lived there. The Miss was evil, and we all knew it, but she pretended to like us, hoping we'd do anything for her. It worked on some of the girls, and they were the ones who got the bigger jobs out of state, but it didn't work on Mina or me."

Mina cleared her throat and shot Cal a look of understanding. "She's right. The Miss was wicked, but for the women who bought into her girl squad nonsense, they were rewarded. Charlotte was one of them."

"Apparently not any longer," Cal said with a shake of his head.

"I think Charlotte acted like she was, but only as a way to protect herself," Marlise said. "If she only wanted older men, she had to move up the ladder by helping The Miss."

"I wonder how many other women have tried to defect and what happened to them," Roman said.

"I'll ask her."

Cal heard the tremble in her words and noticed how her pen shook on her pad. "You don't have to ask her, Marlise," he said, resting his hand on her shoulder for comfort. "Mina can ask her."

"I said I would ask her." Her tone was fierce and defiant in a way he'd never heard before. His little mouse was becoming a lion.

Cal lifted his hand and held it up. "Whatever you're comfortable doing. In the meantime, everyone should get some rest. Until Marlise can get Charlotte to answer a few more questions, we're looking for a needle in a haystack. Hopefully, she'll feel up to a longer questioning session in a few hours."

Cal waited while everyone filed out of the room, but he held Marlise back. Once everyone was gone, he turned to her. "I don't want this to upset you, Mary. If it becomes too much, say the word, and I'll have Mina take over."

He noticed her stiffen, and she took a step closer to him before speaking. "Once again, I'd like to remind you that I'm not a wilting flower, Cal Newfellow. If I ever want my life to be my own again, I have to step up and do the hard stuff too. I know you want to shelter me from having to relive my life when I was held captive, but it might be the only way to be free of it."

He gently grasped her wrist. "But you've come so far since that day you ran onto my plane, and I never want to see you in that kind of shape again. You have to promise me that you'll ask for help if you need it."

She nodded, but Cal couldn't help feeling that she was hiding something. When she picked up her pad and left the room, he stared after her, but his mind was stuck on that scene on the plane the first time he saw her. Their eyes had met, and hers were filled with bottomless terror that he'd felt in the pit of his stomach. He knew that kind of terror, and seeing someone like her experiencing it raised a shield of protectiveness inside him. He wanted to give her room to grow and breathe now that she was out of that situation, but her time with The Madame came back to haunt them every time he tried. She could work for Secure One with no expiration date, but Marlise deserved the chance to experience freedom.

Real freedom. Not protection disguised as freedom. Sure, Marlise knew she could leave Secure One at any time, but she wouldn't survive a week unless The Madame was behind bars and The Miss was caught.

Chapter Eight

Marlise paced her room, but stopped by the adjoining door each time, only to turn away before she knocked. She didn't know what to do. Maybe she should wait to talk to Cal in hopes Charlotte could answer their questions. If Charlotte could tell them where The Miss was, she wouldn't have to upset Cal. If she told him what she'd been hiding and he got upset, he might cut her loose from the lodge, and she wouldn't live through the night.

Another trip around the room had her convinced he wouldn't do that, but she wasn't convinced he would ever talk to her again once he found out the truth. Maybe that was okay. Then she wouldn't have to fight this constant attraction she felt for him. She couldn't explain it, but every time he took her shoulders and stared into her eyes, it was like he was trying to fight the same battle.

Exhausted, she plopped down on her bed and sighed. She had to tell Cal. Maybe it wouldn't matter, but she'd never know if she didn't come clean with him. Marlise pushed herself up, walked to the door and raised her fist. After a short pep talk, she knocked on the adjoining door. He said they should get some rest, so she hoped he had taken his own advice and was in his room. Since she'd come to stay here, everyone said he was different. He was happier and didn't work everyone past exhaustion. She chalked it up to his brother moving here when she did, which meant Cal was happier having family close again, but Mina just rolled her eyes at that response.

When Cal didn't answer the door right away, she lowered her arm, ready to give up for the day, but the swish of the door opening ran a shiver up her spine. His whispered "Mary" in a sleepy voice ratcheted her heart rate up a few notches.

"I'm sorry I woke yo—" She'd spun around to see Cal standing before her wearing nothing but a pair of basketball shorts. Marlise begged her mind to work, but it wouldn't form a sentence. Her brain was too busy snapping images of his tatted chest. She could never have imagined what he was hiding under his tight T-shirts. His chest sported an image of Zeus and Leto, side by side. Zeus was gazing at Leto with admiration, while all around them, storm clouds gathered and lightning bolts rained down.

On an inhaled breath, she took a step closer. One of those lightning bolts followed a jagged scar down his chest. Her finger traced the bumpy skin, and his muscles rippled under her touch. "Your hand wasn't your only injury from the war."

Cal's hand had been injured in a car bomb, and that had ended his military career. They'd saved his hand, but he'd lost two fingers at the middle joint. He had a special prosthesis he wore on his hand that filled in for the missing digits. She didn't even notice it anymore, but this injury was new, and the jagged scar that ended in a round one told her it had involved a bullet.

"A long time ago, Mary," he whispered, capturing her hand and lowering it, but he didn't let go. "Did you need something?"

"What happened, Cal?"

"Why do you care?" he asked, his head tipped in confusion.

"We're all scarred," she said with a shrug. "I wish I could turn my scars into something beautiful like yours."

"You are beautiful, Mary," he whispered, his gaze sweeping the length of her without hesitating for even a moment on her scarred skin. "You don't need ink to make it so."

"How can this be beautiful?" she asked, flicking her hand at her scarred face and arm.

"It's beautiful because you are, and the scars are a beautiful reminder that you survived and thrived despite what someone else inflicted on you. Don't ever, ever tell yourself you're anything but beautiful."

If only that were possible, Marlise thought. He might say she was beautiful, but he didn't have to look at her every day. At least not in a romantic way, but then a man like Cal Newfellow would never consider her a romantic companion. She doubted any man would. Her scars went far deeper than her skin, and sometimes those scars were harder to hide. Working for Cal had taught her to trust him, but once out in the real world, she'd have to protect herself from men who wanted to use and abuse her. She'd had enough of that growing up.

"Where did you just go, Mary?" Cal asked, and she snapped her gaze back to his.

"I—I was just thinking about dangerous men."

"I'm not dangerous, Mary."

"Oh, but you are, Cal. Physically, emotionally and vocationally, you are the most dangerous man in my life. You have the power to put me back into The Miss's line of fire."

Marlise wrung her hands and turned her back to him, walking to the other side of the room. There was no way she could tell him the truth about Red Rye. He would get angry and send her away, but the image of Charlotte sobbing and alone drifted through her mind. It wasn't unlike the memory she had of herself in the same place a couple years ago. She had to do this for the other girls who were still suffering.

The door clicked closed, and a sigh escaped her lips. Had he left? She turned to see him lounging against the wall, his broad and beautiful chest making her forget why they were there. He needed to put more clothes on if she was ever going to tell him the truth. Cal didn't look to be going anywhere though.

He had one bare foot crossed over the other as he met her gaze.

"Is that why you're afraid to tell me about whatever is bugging you? You know I don't threaten anyone's job as punishment."

"But you might when you find out the truth," she whispered. "I like you, Cal, and I like working here, but I have to help the other girls Charlotte left behind."

She squared her shoulders and inhaled a deep breath as he pushed off the door and strode over to her. Even barefoot, his size was formidable and overwhelming. She wanted to sink back into the bed, but she wouldn't. She had to stand up for herself and all the other girls who couldn't right now.

"I like you too, Mary. You wouldn't have the run of this place if I didn't. Tell me what you think is so bad that I'd kick you out."

She closed her eyes and let the memories of that night wash over her. The voices, screams and thuds filled her head. The smoke clogged her throat, and the wall of flames throbbed at her from all sides. "The night of the fire," she said, her voice choked as she inhaled again, the scent of acrid smoke filling her head. "I was trying to save the girls, Cal." A shiver ran through her, and he took her elbow to help her sit.

"How were you trying to save them? They found you by the front door. Were you running back in instead of out?"

"I had to get out. The smoke and the flames, Cal, they were everywhere."

"It must have been disorienting to be inside that kind of fire. Were you trying to get to Mina?"

"No," she whispered. "I was trying to get out!"

"Relax, Mary. I'm trying to figure out how you would save the women."

His warm touch jerked her mind back from the fire, and she focused on him. She was sure he could see the terror in her eyes, but she couldn't stop now. She had to convince him to help her.

"In Red Rye, I did what I wanted without anyone taking notice. I was expendable."

"No." His voice was firm, but there was a steel edge to it. "You are not and never were expendable, Mary."

"To them, I was, Cal. I knew it. Mina knew it. All the girls knew it. I think that's why they talked to me."

"Talked to you?" he asked as he dropped to one knee in front of her.

"More like confided in me," she explained, rubbing the scarred skin on her hand. "They told me things about their dates, and…" Her voice dropped to a whisper as she leaned into his ear, "I recorded it."

Cal's eyes widened at her admittance. "You recorded the conversations? On the computer?"

"No!" she exclaimed. "I'm not dumb, Cal!"

He rubbed her arms up and down to calm her, the metal of his prosthesis cold against her skin. There was something uniquely Cal about it though. "I didn't say you were. If not on a computer, then where?"

"When I first started doing all the grocery shopping and errands, The Miss always sent one of her guards with me to 'help.'"

"But it was to make sure you didn't run?" he asked, and she nodded.

"Eventually, they knew I wasn't going to run because I had no money to do it."

"You weren't getting paid to take care of the house?"

"No. I got to live there and eat. The Miss said that's all she would allow since I wasn't bringing in any money."

"If I ever find this woman…"

Marlise took his hand and offered him a sly grin. "I got her in the end though, Cal. It was easy to siphon money off the cash she'd give me for groceries. I bought a smartphone one day but never activated it. I just used it to hold pictures and recordings. Then I rented a post office box to keep it safe. That's where I was going the night of the fire."

"The post office?"

After a nod and rough swallow, she admitted something she never thought she'd tell another soul. "All the girls told me things about their trips, the men and The Miss. When one phone was full, I bought another."

"You don't have to whisper, Mary. No one here is out to hurt you."

"I don't want you to be upset," she said, jumping up and walking to the other side of the room. "I should have told you sooner, but I was scared and didn't think it mattered."

"What changed that makes you think it matters now?" he asked, rising to his full height of six feet three inches. He was taller than her by a foot. She should have been scared of him, but all she wanted was to be wrapped in his arms. She didn't trust most men after what happened in her life, but she trusted Cal.

She trusted Cal.

That thought stopped her in her tracks. She was twenty-eight years old, and for the first time in her life, she trusted a man.

"I trust you, Cal," she blurted out. He didn't say anything. He just rested his hands on her shoulders and squeezed them. It was like he knew how big of an admittance that was for her. "I trust you, and that's why I'm telling you about the phones. The lawyer on television said there's no such thing as a perfect witness." She flipped around to face him. "Maybe there isn't, but I could be as close to perfect as they come since my past is gone. If I can get the phones, I could testify against The Miss and The Madame!"

"The recordings would help the case, but the lawyers will say they were gathered illegally and therefore not admissible in court."

Marlise paced away from him and then back again, worry filling her that maybe he was right. "I wondered the same thing, but I searched the internet when I lived at the group home, and it said as long as one person in the conversation gives consent, then it's a legal recording that can be played in court."

Cal's lips pursed, and he dipped his head in question. "I can ask Mina or Roman. They'd know, but I'm not sure the recordings would add anything to the pending case against The Madame. The risk to reward is too high. I'm sorry, Mary."

"No, just listen, Cal!" she exclaimed, running to him and planting her hands on Zeus and Leto. "The recordings can answer some of the questions that no one else can."

His hands came around her wrists and held them, his brown eyes almost black in the dim light of her room. "Such as?"

"The cities they most often went to on dates, for starters. If you can just get me to Red Rye, I promise they're worth the time."

"Absolutely not," Cal said, his voice dark and heavy. He pushed her hands away from his chest before he set his jaw. "You'll never step foot back in that town. I'll discuss it with Mina and Roman, and if they think it's worth the risk, I'll send my men. End of story."

"That's impossible, Cal. I have to go."

"No!"

Initially, she stepped back, scared by his fierceness, until she remembered he wouldn't hurt her. He'd already shown that a million times over. She advanced on him instead, and they stood chest to chest.

"Yes. I don't have the key anymore since the house burned down. The only way to get into that box is with my face."

A curse word fell from Cal's lips, and she cocked

a brow, waiting for him to say something else. When he didn't, she played her final trump card.

"Those phones also hold real recordings of The Miss as well as a photo of her."

He leaned forward to hear her better. "Did you just say you have her photo?" Marlise nodded as she swallowed around the lump of fear that was trying to keep her secrets inside. "Why didn't you mention this sooner, Mary?"

The tone of his voice told her he was angry, and she shrank back against the bed for a moment. Then she remembered she had the right to defend herself and her choices just like he did. She stood, ready for battle.

"What good would it have done, Cal? They caught The Madame, and we had no idea where The Miss was or if she was even in business anymore."

"If I had known you had a photo, I could have found her!"

"How?" Marlise exclaimed, her arms going up in the air. "We're more of a ghost than you are, Cal!"

"Why did you take her picture if you knew it was useless?" This time, he asked the question without anger, but rather in confusion.

"I had no idea that we didn't exist in any database when I took it. Once the FBI told me that, the picture of The Miss became useless, at least in my mind. Now, I'm not so sure."

"What do you mean?"

"Well, maybe, if we figure out where she is, the

image will help us find her. I don't know, okay?" she asked, frustrated. "Something is telling me to get the phones. That's what I was trying to do the night of the fire, but I never made it out of the house!"

He turned away from her, his hand in his hair, and she noticed his shoulders rise and fall once. "I can't risk taking you back there, Mary. It's too dangerous!"

"Cal, I can handle myself. Besides, we know The Miss is nowhere near Red Rye."

"Haven't you learned anything?" He hissed the question more than he asked it. "Now that Charlotte is here, The Miss also knows you're here!"

"All the more reason to leave." Her raised brow did nothing to goad him, so she stepped into his space again and rested her hand on his arm. She wanted to put her hands all over his hard chest, but she knew there was only one way that could end, and it wouldn't be in her favor. "The Miss has been gone from Red Rye for two years. There's no way she has anyone local on the payroll."

"You can't be sure of that," he insisted. "I can promise you she's got someone on her payroll there. You going there can't happen."

"It has to happen, Cal. I only paid for three years on the post office box, and my time is almost up. There's no other way to get into the box either. You can't break into a post office and not get caught."

"I'm a ghost, Mary. I can be in and out of a place before anyone is the wiser."

"Not in Red Rye," she said, standing her ground

with crossed arms. "It's a hub. Someone is always there sorting mail and loading trucks."

She tried not to take joy in his grimace, but a tiny part of her enjoyed playing that card.

"Stay put. I need to talk to my people." He strode to the door and yanked it open.

"Fine, but I'm not telling you the box number unless I'm along for the ride!"

The door slammed behind him, telling her exactly what he thought of the gauntlet she'd thrown down.

CAL'S THOUGHTS WERE as dark and dangerous as the lake that spread out before him. He was still reeling from the bombshell Marlise had dropped on him. She'd had ample opportunity to mention the hidden information, but she hadn't. He paced the dock, wishing the lights weren't on so he could hide in the darkness. Instead, his lakeshore was lit up with security lights to warn anyone they wouldn't be taken by surprise. No one took Secure One by surprise anymore.

"You better have a beer in your hand," he called out to his brother as he approached from the lodge.

"Do I look stupid?" Roman asked when he joined him on the dock and handed him a bottle.

Cal looked him up and down as he pulled the cap off the beer. "You want me to answer that?"

Roman shoved him in the shoulder with laughter before bringing the bottle to his lips. "Everything status quo out here?"

"As far as I can tell," Cal said. "All the alarms are

silent, and there's been no movement. I'm inclined to believe Charlotte when she said the other three women left."

Roman nodded, but didn't speak as he stared out over the lake. "You know they're going to attack by air, right?"

"Yep," he agreed, acid swirling in his gut. "It's their only option, but I'm not convinced they have the ability to come in by air. She's sending scared women in to do recon. My confidence is low that she could get a plan together to attack."

"Facts. We still need to assume she can and be prepared though."

"I would like you and Mina to move into the guest room in the lodge. She's still hot, and you know The Miss would take her as fast as she'd take Marlise."

"Something we both agree on," Roman said. "We'll sleep there, but we're spending most of our time in the control room. If you want my opinion, you should go to Red Rye."

Cal grunted rather than answered, and Roman laughed, but his head shook. Whatever he was thinking, Cal didn't want to hear it.

"I think you have a screw loose. Red Rye is dead to us."

Roman's shrug said he didn't believe him, which annoyed Cal. "I know how hard it is to put someone you care about in danger to further a case, but from what Marlise told us while you were out here brooding, the information in the post office box might be worth the risk."

"How?" Cal asked, his arms going up in the air as beer flew across the dock. "Okay, so we know what The Miss looks like, so what? Marlise, Mina and Charlotte do too. That doesn't help us when she's untraceable."

"We could run her voice through our programs and see if we get a hit."

"I don't think she's doing television or radio interviews, Roman." Cal sat, and exhaustion hung like a cloak across his shoulders.

"Maybe not," Roman said, sitting next to him, "but that doesn't mean she didn't in her past life. The recordings might give us information about where to find the woman."

"It's unlikely that any of the women knew her bug out plan."

Roman pointed at him as he finished his beer and set it on the dock by his feet. "That's true, but have you considered human nature in this situation?"

Cal stared at him in confusion. He wasn't processing things as fast as he should, and he knew it, but all he could see was a scared Marlise sneaking a phone into the house, likely at great risk to herself, to try and stop what was happening under its roof. Roman grasped his shoulder in a show of brotherly support, almost like he knew Cal needed it. He did, but he would never admit weakness to his brother or anyone else on this property. He was supposed to be steady as a rock and block the blows no matter how hard or fast they came. And he did, except for the blow he took an hour ago. That one hit him out of left field and nearly knocked him out.

"What are you talking about, Roman? I've had two hours of sleep in the last two days. I'm not going to solve riddles."

"It wasn't a riddle," his brother said with a laugh. "It was a genuine question. You say that the women wouldn't know her bug out plan, and that's true, but they knew her, and humans are nothing if not predictable. When we feel threatened, we fall back on the people and places we know best. It's possible that with the information Charlotte can give us, along with those recordings, we might narrow down where The Miss is hiding out."

Cal tipped his head in agreement but stared out over the lake instead of answering. He was stuck between a rock and a hard place. "Risking Marlise's life for 'might' isn't reassuring."

"Might is more than we have right now, Cal. If we want our lives back, we have no choice but to take any chance we have to find The Miss, even if it's the slightest chance."

Cal stood again and set his hands on his hips. "Marlise is refusing to cooperate."

"No, Marlise is trying to take her life back. She's learning to stand up for herself for the first time ever."

"She had to pick me to be the one to stand up to?"

Roman stepped up to him and stuck his finger

in his chest. "Yes, and it's time you stop acting like she's putting you out because of it. She picked you for a reason."

"I'm convenient."

"No," Roman said with a shake of his head. "You're safe. It's taken her two years to learn to trust a man, but your tirade is setting her right back where she was when we brought her here."

"What does that mean?" Cal asked with his jaw clenched. When Marlise arrived at Secure One, she was timid, scared and afraid to do anything that might upset him.

"She's inside the lodge asking Charlotte questions, trying to get more information. I overheard her tell Mina she would do anything to find The Miss so your life could go back to normal. She thinks you feel responsible for her because she's damaged." Cal opened his mouth, but Roman held up a finger. "Those were her exact words. She wants to be part of Secure One and not just as a support person who cooks and cleans for the team."

"Everyone is part of the team at Secure One," Cal said. "No one is any better than anyone else here, and you know it."

"You're missing the point, Cal. Marlise needs to be part of finding the woman who tried to kill her, not hide while other people do it."

"She needs to take her power back."

"Yes!" Roman exclaimed with laughter. "Finally. She has never had any power in this life, but now she finally does. Those recordings only exist because she took a huge risk to make them."

"And now she's the only one with the power to retrieve them."

Roman pointed at him. "I've known Marlise for years, and I'll tell you this, she's firm on her decision to be the only one who goes to Red Rye. Accept it, or don't, that's your choice, but you will damage her confidence by refusing to talk to her. Just think about it."

Roman turned and walked away, leaving Cal to stare after him while his words echoed in his ears. Marlise's power had been taken away at birth, first by her birth parents and then by her foster parents. That dictated the path for the rest of her life. Then she came to Secure One, and he gave her back the power to decide what she did, how she did it and when she did it. He gave her back the power to take care of herself by teaching her self-defense and how to use a gun. He gave her power by asking her to talk to Charlotte and ask the critical questions.

Cal swore as he jogged toward the lodge. Roman was right. He'd been the one to teach her how to harness her power, and he couldn't be the one to take it away. He had to get her to Red Rye, no matter what it cost him.

Chapter Nine

Marlise sat next to Charlotte and held her hand. She was still in the med bay so Selina could keep an eye on her, but she was determined to get more information about The Miss's operation for Cal. If she could, maybe he'd see she was a valuable member of the team and consider taking her to get the phones she'd hidden. The look on Cal's face when she told him about the post office box crossed her mind, and she grimaced. Chances were good he might never speak to her again, much less take her back to Red Rye.

"Are you feeling better?" Marlise asked the woman who reminded her so much of herself just a few years ago. Charlotte was depressed, angry and terrified, but Marlise could see the relief in her as well. She wasn't here as a pawn in a game. She'd found a way out and took it.

"I'm sorry that I lost it earlier. The memories, sometimes they swamp me, and I can't force the emotions down."

"You don't have to apologize," Marlise promised.

"I remember living there. Working for The Madame has lifelong effects, but it does get better. I'm proof of that."

"I know," Charlotte agreed with a wan smile. "I always looked up to you, Marlise. You knew how to work the room, so to say, and keep yourself safe. I told myself if I ever got a chance to run, I would be as brave as you were."

"I wasn't brave," Marlise said with a shake of her head. "I was trapped in the house and almost died. I got lucky and only survived because Roman found me. A few more minutes in that house, and I wouldn't be sitting here right now."

Charlotte shrugged as she toyed with the mug in front of her. "Maybe, but you're working here now and trying to shut her down. I want to be part of that."

"Good," Marlise said, squeezing her hand. "I have a few more questions."

"I'll try, but I know so little." Charlotte shook her head and sucked in a deep breath.

"Sometimes we know more than we think we do," Marlise reminded her. "For instance, can you tell me what cities The Miss sent you to for dates when in Red Rye?"

Her mouth twisted to the side, and she glanced up at the ceiling as though she had to think about it. "I had only been on three of them before the fire, and two were in Kansas City. The third one was probably in Texas, though I wasn't told where. I was in a hotel the whole time. Maybe Dallas? I wasn't privy to any documents with an address."

"I wondered about that since you weren't doing it for long before the fire. What about the other girls? Emelia and Bethany, where were they sent?"

"I don't know. We weren't allowed to talk about it, and we didn't. We were too afraid The Miss would overhear and call us out."

Marlise nodded, but she was thinking about the phones again in Red Rye. She wondered why the girls talked to her without fear. Maybe it wasn't that they were afraid of The Miss, but they were afraid one of the other girls would try to home in on their clients. Then again, maybe they were afraid someone would narc to The Miss about them to get a better standing with her. Marlise couldn't remember all of the cities and what girls went where. Not without listening to the recordings, at least. She struggled to remember a lot of things about her life in Red Rye before the fire. "One question the team had was, how is The Miss paying for all of this? Does she pay the girls?"

"She was confiscating bundles of money in Red Rye when we returned from our dates. She kept them in the safe at the house. I think she also trafficked drugs that The Madame didn't know about."

"She was siphoning off The Madame to set up her own business."

"Absolutely. The Miss believed she was a better leader than The Madame. It was only a matter of time before she tried to part ways and do her own thing. The fire at Red Rye accelerated her plan, but she had the money to get what she needed quickly. As for paying us, she doesn't. If she paid us, we'd have money and might try to run. Our payment is room and board. The Miss is incredibly paranoid. She doesn't let us off the property without a blindfold and a guard. She even has some male guards now. When girls return from dates—" she put the word in quotation marks "—they turn over the money to her immediately."

"If you have to be blindfolded, how did you get to Secure One? How did you even know I was here?"

"We get to take the blindfolds off once the plane is in the air. We can't see out the windows anyway. Once we landed, a car was waiting, and we followed the preprogrammed GPS."

"You're saying that she doesn't want you to know where home base is, so if you're captured, you can't talk."

Charlotte pointed at her with a nod.

"Does she send a guard? How else can she assure that you don't defect?"

The other woman was quiet while she stared at her lap. Whatever the answer to that question was, it took a toll on her.

"There was a guard with us. If anyone tried to run, they'd be—" she glanced up at Mack before she dropped her gaze again to her lap "—shot." The whispered word ran a shiver up Marlise's spine.

"You said it was a bad idea for a girl to say no. Is that what happens if they do?" Her nod was immediate, but her hand came to her mouth to cover it. Marlise wasn't sure if she was going to be sick or was trying not to sob.

"Emelia and Bethany tried to say no, and we haven't seen them since."

Marlise lifted a brow in surprise. "Emelia and Bethany were her top girls in Red Rye."

"They were, and they didn't like how they were treated once we got to the new place. They decided they wanted more of the pie and challenged The Miss. If you ask me, she made them an example for the rest of us."

"If you challenge her, you're buried."

Marlise worried about what would happen when the other three girls returned to home base without Charlotte. Chances were good they'd be buried too.

"We didn't know why we were sent here until I heard on the radio in the car that the trial for The Madame had been postponed because someone tried to kill the lead witness. I might not have a college degree, but I'm smart enough to know you were one of the lead witnesses. Once I heard that, I knew The Miss had failed to get rid of you and had to make a new plan."

"I wonder how she knew I was at Secure One."

"She talked nonstop about the plane you took off on a few years ago, and she finally figured out who it belonged to."

"What were you supposed to do when you got here?"

"The guard had to take pictures and draw maps of the property with entry points for the team that would follow us."

"There are no entry points," Marlise said with a shake of her head. "Secure One is a fortress now."

"Which we figured out quickly. That was why I had to convince the other girls to let me try to infiltrate via the lakeshore. The guard was new, and she was as overwhelmed as we were. She said I could, but they'd leave without me if I didn't return to the car by a set time. She reminded me that meant I could never find my way back to The Miss, but The Miss would find me and kill me if I defected."

With a cocked brow, Marlise asked, "How would she find you?"

Charlotte leaned forward and whispered into Marlise's ear. "My tracker."

Marlise's eyes widened, and she leaned forward so Mack couldn't hear her. "You have a tracker?"

She nodded, and Marlise could read the terror in her eyes. "I cut it out and buried it in the sand." Her whispered confession was tearful and told Marlise of the level of paranoia The Miss had reached since leaving Red Rye. "Once the battery is dead, she'll think I am too."

She held up a finger to Charlotte and walked over to Mack. "Do they make trackers small enough to implant in humans?"

"No, not that I'm aware of," Mack said, his gaze flicking to Charlotte for a moment. "Why?"

"Charlotte said The Miss had a tracker in her. She cut it out and left it on the beach."

Mack's brows went up in tandem. "They make small ones for purses, but still over an inch thick. I suppose you could implant it, but it would be painful. The battery isn't going to last longer than a couple of days."

Marlise walked back to Charlotte. "When did she put in the tracker?"

"Right before we left. She put it under the skin and sewed it up. It was so painful, and we had to try to walk through the woods with it in our legs. She said they'd keep us honest because she could track our movements."

"Is that the wound they found in your thigh when they searched you?" Charlotte nodded, and Marlise sighed.

"I was glad I got rid of it before Cal captured me since they searched for a tracker."

"The Miss will either think you're dead or a hostage now."

"Or that I defected. Regardless of what The Miss thinks, I doubt she will bother with me. She wants to stop you from testifying. Nothing else matters."

"I need to talk to Mary." Cal's voice was loud from the door where Mack stood. Mack whispered something, and then Cal's voice boomed through the hallway. "I don't have time to wait on this, Mack!"

Marlise stood and squeezed Charlotte's hand. "I'll be back. Rest now, and let Selina know if you need anything for pain."

Charlotte nodded with a sad smile. "Thanks, Marlise. Be careful. She's hell-bent on stopping you from testifying any way she can. She just has to find you first."

"I've got one of the best teams looking out for me. I'll be fine."

Marlise turned and walked to the door to deal with her team leader. His attitude with Mack told her he was back in work mode. She had some things to tell him, and she hoped the information Charlotte gave her would tip the scales in her favor and get them back to Red Rye.

"ROMAN SAYS MISSION ACCOMPLISHED. Be careful and follow the plan." Marlise's voice filled the quiet car.

"Tell them ten-four and to keep us in their sights." She nodded and typed his response out to Roman.

At least that was one problem solved. Roman and Mina had found Charlotte's tracker on the beach, driven it out to a lake in the middle of nowhere several hours from Secure One and buried it on the lakeshore. Once The Miss triangulated on the location and figured out it was a lake, she would hopefully believe that Charlotte was dead and no longer a threat. Hopefully. There was no guarantee, but it was the best way to buy time if nothing else.

After a long and complicated planning meeting

and a night of sleep, they waited for dark to descend and then headed south to Red Rye, hoping the phones Marlise had stashed could break the case wide-open. Cal wasn't convinced, but he trusted her instincts. He hadn't heard the recordings, so he couldn't say they wouldn't be helpful until he did.

He glanced over at the woman in the passenger seat. Their plan was tricky. They'd left Secure One in a dummy van and switched cars two hours later. They'd drive their current vehicle into Red Rye as soon as the post office opened, and Marlise would get the phones from the box. Once they had them, they'd transfer cars again and drive west several hours to a hotel. If they didn't pick up a tail from Red Rye, they'd switch cars and drive back to Secure One during the night.

"I wish we could have taken the helicopter." Marlise sighed. "This is tense."

Cal squeezed her shoulder for a moment before putting his hand back on the wheel. "I know, but taking any mode of transportation that could be traced back to Secure One was too risky. The Miss tagged my plane, which means she knows my chopper too."

Cal didn't say how angry he was that The Miss had found Marlise because of him. Once again, he'd failed to offer the protection his entire business was based around. Instead, he'd led bad people to good people not once but twice. Secure One. What a joke. He was the least secure one in the area, and The Madame and The Miss were the ones to teach him that both times.

"And you don't think a van with a fake technology repair logo will trick someone watching?"

"You'd be surprised how easy it is to overlook the obvious. I run a company that depends on technology. Besides, I don't believe The Miss is monitoring Secure One. She doesn't have the manpower."

"More like woman power," Marlise corrected him.

She was right. If The Miss was running this operation with scared women and no one else, then going to Red Rye was worth the risk. Charlotte did say that there were male guards now, but she didn't know how many. If The Miss had enough, she might send them to Minnesota to attack Secure One. Better to find her before they showed up.

He didn't like that they had no backup, but Roman was right. The more cars in play, the greater risk of showing up on someone's radar. It was up to him to keep Marlise safe, and he'd die to make sure she didn't. He shook his head to clear his thoughts. Did he just think that? He'd never thought that about a woman before—not even when Mina had been kidnapped.

Mina was Roman's. Marlise is yours.

No. That was not an option. He had led The Miss to their door. He should have taken more time to develop a better plan, but they didn't have time on their side two years ago. The Madame had forced their hand. And this time, The Miss was forcing it. His jaw pulsed with the internal anger he had toward himself for even thinking he could be with someone again. Being with someone was dangerous, and an excellent way to get your heart broken or someone killed. He had learned that the hard way. While he was on this side of the grave, he would never take that risk again.

Marlise held up the small device in her hand. It was bigger than a cell phone but smaller than an iPad and allowed them to communicate with Secure One on a dedicated line. The information stayed on the screen for only three minutes before it disappeared. It was a solid way to get information back and forth when a team member was in the field without risking it falling into the wrong hands.

"Mina finished her deep dive into the Red Rye postmaster. From what she can see, he's squeaky clean. There were no large deposits made in his accounts, and she couldn't find any gambling debts or communication with anyone she couldn't validate. He has several car loans, credit card balances and a mortgage. She doesn't think he's on any payroll other than the US government's. At least not that she can find."

Cal pointed at her. "That's the important caveat. He could be on the payroll but paid in cash. We'll have to trust that Mina's information is correct, but we need to get in and out fast just in case. Since Red Rye is a hub, it means there will be a lot of employees, and we can't check them all."

"That's true," she agreed, "but the sorting will be mostly done by the time we arrive. We'll only have to deal with the postmaster. I know it's a risk, Cal, but Mina has done the legwork to minimize it as much as possible."

Cal set his jaw and kept the van hurtling down the highway. The sun was coming up, and they'd have to stop soon and use the facilities. He glanced at the clock. It was almost 6:00 a.m. They had an hour left to drive and then an hour to surveil the post office before it opened to the public. He refused to get his hopes up for an uncomplicated mission. Nothing ever went according to plan when The Miss or The Madame was involved. He had to stay two steps ahead of them.

"We have to find this woman and stop her."

Marlise's hand clamped around his giant forearm, and he swallowed down the sensation of solidarity it gave him. He could not fall for this woman. Once they found The Miss, Marlise had to be free to live her life for herself. She couldn't be tied to him emotionally or financially. She deserved to make her own choices independent of him once this psychopath was found and stopped.

"I know you think this is a bad idea, but thank you for taking the chance on me. I won't let you down."

The air left his chest in a whoosh. "Mary, you could never let me down."

"I'd be more convinced if you hadn't stormed out of my room when I told you about the phones."

"I'm sorry about that," he said, running a hand down his face. "The information took me by surprise. It had been years since you left Red Rye, and you never mentioned it."

"I didn't think they mattered," she said, and he could hear the pleading in her voice. "I wasn't withholding them on purpose. They were just a dead end in my mind until Charlotte arrived and told us The Miss had built a new empire."

"Then suddenly those old phones became important."

"At least I hope so, because I know how big of a risk we're taking, Cal."

"Nothing ventured, nothing gained."

A head shake accompanied her snort of laughter. "That is not a motto Cal Newfellow lives by, but nice try."

"You think you know a lot about me."

"You aren't that hard to figure out, Cal. Something happened in the military that you don't talk about now. I respect that. There are things I don't talk about either. Whatever happened is the reason you started Secure One. You want to protect people from the bad guys and go to any lengths to ensure it. You consider everyone at Secure One family rather than employees."

"In the army, every member of your team is a brother. I built my business the same way."

"Why Secure One then? That's incredibly singular."

He didn't answer as he neared the rest area where they'd stop and prepare to make their only move on the board. He pulled into the empty parking lot, chosen because it was nothing more than a small building on the side of the road with plenty of trees to hide their vehicle. They would stay hidden until it was time to finish their drive back into hell.

Once he'd put the car into Park, he turned to her. "Secure one was the last thing I said to the only woman I've ever loved. It meant the area was secure, and it was safe to move. It wasn't secure, and she paid the price. I named my business Secure One so I'd never make that mistake again."

"Falling in love or not securing an area?" she asked, her gaze intent upon him.

"Both."

Without a backward glance, he climbed from the car to prepare for the next mission.

Chapter Ten

Secure one was the last thing I said to the only woman I've ever loved.

The words hadn't left Marlise's mind since Cal had uttered them an hour ago. Since then, he'd done nothing but bark orders at her like she was a soldier on his team. She tried not to take offense to it. He had opened up to her, and she knew how difficult that was for him. She understood it on a personal level most people wouldn't. Whatever happened the day his girlfriend died wasn't all on his shoulders though. When it came to the military, it was never up to one person to secure an area. That was why they had teams. Regardless, Cal was the kind of guy who would bear the burden of any failure so the rest of his team didn't have to. While she understood it, she hated it for him. No one should live that way.

"I killed a man once," she admitted. Did she say that aloud? She threw a hand over her mouth and hoped he didn't hear her.

His hands froze on the straps of his vest. He was

standing in front of her and, in another breath, pushed her back against the car. "Excuse me?"

"I'm sorry. I shouldn't have said that." A tear ran down her cheek, brought about by the admittance and the guilt. "I didn't mean to say that out loud."

Her whispered confession softened him, and he pulled her into a hug. "Something tells me you didn't mean to kill him."

"He was assaulting me," she said in a choked whisper. "If I didn't get him off me, I would die. All I had within reach was a shiv. I accidentally hit his carotid, and he bled out."

"I'm sorry, Mary. I wouldn't wish that kind of experience on anyone."

"You're not alone, Cal. There are a lot of experiences I don't talk about either. You were in the military and probably saw many horrible things, but they don't define you. You're a good person who takes care of your family without hesitation. Whatever happened to your friend was a series of unfortunate events but not your fault. There's a chain of command in the military for a reason."

"You don't know any such thing, Mary. You've never been in war."

"That's not true," she said, pushing him away. "A war is a war, whether it's fought on the street or on foreign soil. You do things in war you would never do in peacetime. No one understands that better than me, Cal," she said, poking herself in the chest. "Don't tell me I've never fought for my life or for something I believed in because you don't know that!" This time, her finger went into his chest, and he closed his fist around it, the metal and rubber fingers clacking as they closed.

"I'm sorry. You know that wasn't what I meant. I simply meant that if you haven't been in the military, you don't understand the intricacies of the missions. I dropped the ball."

"Did you though? Have you taken the time to consider that maybe someone else dropped the ball, and the game was over long before you got on the field? You'll never find peace until you consider that as a possibility, Cal. You're too damn young to sit around brooding for the rest of your life because of one mistake."

"That mistake cost a woman her life!" he ground out.

"But was it your mistake?" she quietly asked. "Really think about it. I've known you for two years, and you're meticulous when you run a mission. You're not like that because of what happened to her. That's your personality and who you are as a person. Have you ever considered that what happened that day wasn't your fault?"

"Absolutely not," he said, his gaze pinned on hers. "I was the team leader, so the mission failure was on me. My intel was bad, but I should have approached things differently. I should have held the team back until I knew for sure. I should have done something more than I did."

"You were given bad information, followed orders, and the mission failed. That's tragic, but that doesn't make it your fault."

Cal slid his hand up her cheek as they stood in the early air of a cool October morning. "Hannah's death will always be on my hands, Mary."

She grasped his wrist and stopped his hand from touching her scarred cheek. "Do you think Hannah would feel that way if she were here? I wasn't in the military, but there isn't a veteran who won't tell you they knew the risks when they signed up. What would Hannah think if she knew your life revolved around her death? Would that make her happy? Would she take comfort or joy in knowing you punish yourself every day for her death?"

Cal's gaze was so intense she was afraid she would combust under it, but what she saw in his eyes scared her the most. He truly believed he had killed the woman he loved, and she would never convince him otherwise. He needed to stop beating himself up for something that went beyond the scope of his job that day.

Slowly, his hand slipped from her face, and he took a step back without saying anything. Cal Newfellow was a crypt, and he couldn't make it clearer that she was not the keeper.

He pulled the car door open and motioned her in. "Are you ready for the resurgence at Red Rye?"

Was she ready? As she lowered herself to the car seat, the answer was easy. No, but she didn't have the luxury of time. If she wanted her life back, she would have to do the hard work, which started back where it all began.

Red Rye, Kansas. Population: four thousand.

WHEN SHE NOTICED her reflection in the post office door, she was glad her coat hid her bulletproof vest. At least she had that going for her. Her fingers played with her blond hair before she took a breath and pulled the door open. Being back in Red Rye hit her in a way she hadn't expected. She'd expected the anxiety to hit hard and brutal. Admittedly, she was anxious to get the phones and get out of town, but that was the only anxiety filling her belly. She was pleasantly numb to any other emotion as she walked into the lobby of the place she had once considered a fortress for her secrets. Once she left here, they wouldn't be secrets for long.

Cal had her back, but now that she was inside, she was on her own in retrieving the phones. They'd been watching the post office for an hour, and nothing seemed amiss, according to Cal, but then The Miss was never obvious. Subtle is your middle name when you're running an illegal prostitution ring smack-dab in the middle of a small town.

With a glance behind her, she made eye contact with Cal. He was loitering outside the door, pretending to smoke a cigarette. His head was on a swivel though, as he "took in the town's charm."

After a deep breath, she approached the counter,

grateful Roland was still the postmaster. He was always so kind to her when she lived here.

"Marlise!" he exclaimed the moment he laid eyes on her. "Well, I never thought I'd see you again! But here you are."

"Hi, Roland," she answered, though her voice wavered. She cleared her throat before she spoke again. "I wanted to pick up my mail before my box expired. Unfortunately, I no longer have the key. You know, after the fire and everything."

"Oh, sure, sure," he said, nodding as though he didn't want to bring up the way the town had been tainted by The Madame either. "I'm happy to get it for you."

She held a bag out to him. "You can use this. Thank you."

The postmaster took the bag with a smile and walked back behind the bank of post office boxes. There would be no mail, only the cell phones. She prayed they'd still charge so they could access the information. Cal told her to act casual, as though it were any other day, and she was simply picking up her mail. She didn't know how hard that would be until she stood there exposed. She forced herself to remain calm as she waited, but he needed to hurry.

There was a bounty out on her head, and if she didn't find a way to stop The Miss, she wouldn't have one. The thought sent a shiver down her spine. The Miss would love nothing more than to have her head, but Marlise had worked too hard and suffered too much to fall back into that woman's grasp.

"Not much in there considering how long you were gone," the postmaster said, jarring Marlise from her thoughts. She jumped but covered it by reaching for the bag.

"I'm sure not. I changed my address immediately when I moved. Thanks again for getting this for me," she said, holding up the bag. "You can let the box go now. I won't be back."

"I'm sorry to see you go, Marlise, but I understand. What happened to you here in Red Rye was terrible. Don't be a stranger if you ever find yourself this way again."

Marlise thanked him and waved before she headed for the door. Not a chance she'd step foot in Red Rye again. This was her past. Her future was out there to find once The Miss was captured. Her gaze locked with Cal's, and she wished for a moment that he were her future. He was the kind of man you trusted without question because there was no doubt in your mind that he'd keep you safe.

Remembering their discussion, she didn't make eye contact on her way past him. She noticed him drop the cigarette and grind it out with his foot before catching up to her, his hands in the pockets of his coat that hid his bulletproof vest. He'd told her to pretend they were a couple on the outs, so she yanked the door open to the car and tossed the bag inside. On a huff, she slid into the passenger seat.

"Did you get them?"

"Yes. Let's get out of here." She donned a pair of sunglasses and crossed her arms over her chest, staring out the window as though she were mad at the man next to her.

The car rumbled as they headed away from the town that had broken her body, mind and spirit. The car was silent and tense until they reached the next county, but when they made it without a tail, she breathed a small sigh of relief. They were still in the race and, with the phones, a few steps closer to the finish line.

"I'm proud of you," he said, glancing at her for a moment.

"For what?" She bent over and tugged a brunette wig over her hair. It wouldn't fool anyone who knew her, but it would fool everyone else.

"You walked into that post office with your head held high and not a nerve in sight. You did what had to be done in a place you wanted to forget. Not everyone can do that."

"Oh, there were nerves," she said with a chuckle. "A whole lot of them."

"You wouldn't have known it, and that's why I'm so proud of you. You've come a long way since Red Rye, baby."

Baby? He didn't mean that as a term of endearment, right? She shook her head at the thought that he meant it exactly like that.

"We've come a long way," she corrected him, offering him a rare smile of genuine happiness. "But we have a few more miles before we can say we crossed the finish line."

His lips pursed, and he nodded. "I know. It doesn't look like we picked up a tail out of Red Rye, which is good. We're still switching out cars before we drive to the hotel. Don't give up. We've got this."

She glanced down at his hand on her shoulder and was suddenly afraid that he got her in a way that went deeper than she might like. She might escape The Miss without further damage to her body, but she'd absolutely leave Secure One with a broken heart.

Chapter Eleven

The walk through the dark streets of Salina, Kansas, had rejuvenated Cal after the long drive from Red Rye. He'd specifically asked for a late and contact-free check-in. They were almost safe for the night, and for that, he was grateful. Once he got them into their room, he'd let Marlise rest while he reached out to Roman at Secure One. He wanted an update on chatter about the trial or The Miss, so he could make a plan to return home. He'd rather not be in the wind with the hottest witness in the country, but he may not have a choice if Secure One was no longer secure.

His disobedient eyes glanced at the woman next to him. She was beautiful as a brunette, but he still preferred her blonde. It was as though she lost her innocence without the blond hair. He was so incredibly proud of her though. They'd been running non-stop for days, but she kept up with him and never complained. He'd been terrified for her when she walked into the post office this morning. Not just about The Miss either. He was worried that being back in Red Rye would trigger memories she couldn't fight through to finish the job. He should have known better. Marlise was tougher than both Roman and him combined.

Cal had been overwhelmed with a feeling that he'd kept tamped down for years, and he'd been breathless for a moment until he pushed it back. He would not fall for another woman, and he certainly wouldn't fall for a woman who was just as headstrong, stubborn and brave as Hannah had been. He forced them both from his mind to concentrate on their next steps. Hotel. Shower. Clean clothes. Food. Recordings. He was anxious to hear and see the woman at the heart of all this chaos.

"Are we almost there?" Marlise muttered next to him.

"Almost," he promised with a smile and tossed his chin at the lights ahead. "A shower and comfy bed are just up ahead. You deserve it." Rather than drive to the hotel, he'd left the rental an hour's walk away at a depot and they'd come in on foot. It was safer that way. If they had to run, they weren't tied to the city grid the way they had been in Minneapolis. On foot, they could go where cars couldn't, and Cal knew if they had to escape, that would be the only way.

"Do you think we're in the clear?" she nervously asked, her gaze flicking around the darkened street as they crossed to their hotel for the night.

"No. I think we're in a lull. The Miss hasn't found

us yet, but she will, and when she does, she will hit us with everything she has. Before that happens, we need to access those recordings, find her and hit her when she's not expecting it."

Marlise was quiet the rest of the way to the hotel room. Because of his late check-in request, the hotel had texted him the room number and code for the side and room door. He wanted to bypass contact with the desk clerk. That mattered to Cal for both their safety and the safety of the innocent people they might come in contact with over the next several days. He punched in the code and pulled the door open with a quick glance around the area, but they were alone. He'd insisted on the room closest to an exit as an escape route as well as to avoid being seen by anyone. Marlise's brunette wig was long, and it hung down over her face to hide her burns. It was harder for him to be unmemorable. His size alone stood out, but there wasn't much he could do about it other than get inside the room as quickly as possible.

"Almost there." Cal pressed in the code for the room, and the light turned green.

He held the door for Marlise, and she slipped through, the heat of her skin brushing against his to remind him of a woman's touch. To remind him of the sensation of holding a woman he cared about in an intimate way. It had been too long since he'd experienced the touch of a woman, but Marlise would not be his next.

You don't mix business with pleasure, Cal.

That little voice gave a hearty guffaw as he secured the door. He ignored it. It could laugh all it wanted, but it would not get the last laugh.

Marlise had stopped in the middle of the room to stare at the king-size bed. "There's only one bed."

Cal was as surprised as she was, but he couldn't let it show. "I asked for a room closest to an exit. I didn't think to ask how many beds." He took her backpack from her shoulder and the hat and wig from her head and set them aside. After he'd straightened her hair, he motioned at the bed. "It's no big deal. One of us can sleep while the other listens to the recordings. Okay?"

"Sure, yeah," she agreed while she nodded. "It's no big deal."

As she gathered her things to shower, he had no doubt in his mind it was a big deal to her. It was a big deal to him too, but he'd never let on, not after their discussion about Hannah earlier. It was a firm reminder that he had better stay in his lane when it came to Marlise, and his lane was not the carpool lane.

WHEN MARLISE FINISHED in the shower, Cal had a pizza and a cold Coke waiting. After they'd eaten, she had to face the phones. She was terrified of them charging and equally terrified of them not charging. If they didn't charge, they were back to square one in the investigation. If they did charge, she'd have to face the woman who'd tried to kill her. She wasn't sure where she'd find the strength to do it.

She glanced at Cal, who was setting up the equipment they would need to listen to the recordings and consult with Secure One. He was her strength. He always stood by her, whether in silent solidarity or to hold her up. He helped her face the trauma from her past life, and she walked away stronger each time.

She yearned to do it by herself though. To rely on herself when the going got tough. Her mind traveled back to Secure One, where Mina sat at a computer while wearing a piece of carbon fiber and steel on what was left of her leg. The Miss had done that to her, and Mina still needed Roman's help when the going got tough. Maybe it was okay that she depended on Cal for moral support?

Don't get used to it, that voice reminded her.

There would be a day when Cal was gone, and she'd have to stand up for herself. She knew it was coming, but for now, for tonight, she'd let him help her through this new wrinkle from her past. After their discussion at the car this morning, she understood him better. He was just as scared as she was. Scared of losing someone again. He kept everyone at arm's length because if he didn't get close to anyone, they wouldn't end up like Hannah. Marlise doubted that he was to blame for her death. A link broke on the chain long before Cal took over the mission, but he was the kind of guy who wouldn't see it. The mission failed, and the woman he loved was dead. That was his fault. It broke her heart to think he lived with that every day.

Wars were ugly. They left carnage and death behind. There was no way to predict what the enemy would do. You just had to be prepared to react when they attacked. Unfortunately for Hannah, she was a casualty of a war she didn't start. The man Marlise had killed was a casualty of a war he chose to start. Someone was always going to lose. Mary had lost a lot in life and so had Marlise, but as Marlise, she saw hope for her future.

"I don't want to go by Mary," she blurted out before slapping her hand over her mouth.

Cal set the tablet he'd been messing with down and walked over to her on the bed. He knelt in front of her. "You've been thinking about it?"

She nodded and swallowed to quell her dry throat. "Mary was someone who suffered a lot in the war on the streets. She did a lot of things Marlise isn't proud of, and that's saying a lot considering who Marlise is."

"And you're speaking about yourself in the third person now." He gave her a wink to tell her he was teasing, but it lifted her lips into a smile. "You do what's right for you. Whether you go by Mary, Marlise or a new name entirely, your past experiences and the people you knew will always be part of you. A name change won't wipe your memories away, even if it wipes away their past from society. Does that make sense?"

"You're right," she admitted, staring down at her hands. "Every experience I've had as far back as I can remember has made me the person I am today. All I know is, I went from Mary to Marlise and, despite being trapped in the sex trade, took a step up in life. Once I figured out how to play The Miss to gain immunity, the stability of Red Rye helped me find even ground for the first time ever. I had plans to put The Miss away, and I worked toward that goal every day. In hindsight, I realize my mistake. I didn't predict how brutal and evil she truly was."

"You couldn't have predicted the fire," he said, taking her hand. "That was set by an agent of the FBI."

"I know, but do you understand what I'm trying to say, Cal?" Her tone was imploring, and he took her other hand with a nod. His thumb rubbed across the scarred tissue of her hand, and she wondered if he even realized that he did it.

"I do understand, and I know whether you go by Mary, Marlise or any other name, you're courageous enough to do anything. You'll put The Miss away for good, so she stops hurting others. If you're ready, we can start to unravel her web of lies so you can have your freedom back."

"What about you?" Marlise asked, her gaze pinned on his handsome face. He was sporting a heavy five o'clock shadow that he was using to his advantage as a disguise.

"What about me?"

"When will you get your freedom back?"

"Never." The word was a rasped whisper, and Marlise shook her head.

"You can't lecture me about being brave enough to take my freedom back if you're unwilling to do the same thing."

He didn't speak or even move. He just knelt there with his gaze so intent it made her insides tremble. This morning when he'd stared at her with the same look in his eyes, she swore he was going to kiss her. There was an internal battle going on behind those eyes. If she had to guess, his steely resolve would win, and he'd put distance between them again. It was his way of beating back the enemy. She wasn't the enemy, even if he saw her as one. The enemy was the voice that told him he didn't deserve to be with anyone again. It told him no one could heal his heart, so it was better not to try. She doubted he ever would. He was too busy taking care of everyone else to worry about his own—

Marlise's thoughts went off the rails when Cal reared up and planted his lips on hers. He grasped the back of her head and kissed her with the hunger and ferocity of a man who had been alone for too long. In her, Cal had found a connection that was undeniably frayed but still holding up to the demand asked of it. Now, he was trying to shore up the connection. Reweave the frayed fibers into a connection he could trust when the time came.

She tipped her head to get closer, to dig deeper. Marlise had dreamed of kissing this man since the first summer she'd lived at Secure One, but he'd hung a do-not-disturb sign long ago. The sign was gone tonight, and his lips were soft as he teased hers. There was the promise of more as his tongue traced the slit of her lips in an unspoken request for entrance. He wanted to be the first to claim the part of her that no man had yet entered. Marlise had been with many men, but she never let them kiss her. That was the only thing she could control back then. She'd wanted to save something for the man who might someday love her despite what all the other men had done to her. Was Cal that man? She doubted it, but her lips parted anyway, giving him the first right to taste her.

When his tongue slipped inside, his heat came with it, and she worried she'd burn up under his lips and hands. It wasn't a bad way to go. His right thumb ran across the scarred flesh of her face as though he were healing it with each caress. Maybe he was. It was easy for Marlise to think he could. When she'd seen the damage to her face and arm for the first time, she'd mourned the last hope that one day some-one would love her.

"Cal," she whispered when he broke the kiss for air.

"I'm sorry," he rasped, running his hand down his face. "I shouldn't have done that."

He tried to turn away, but she grasped his chin and held tight. "Don't run away from me, Cal. I'm not the enemy."

"You're right. I'm my own worst enemy. I'm the reason The Miss found you, and I don't have the right to kiss you!"

"Cal," she said, grasping his shirt so he couldn't turn away. "What are you talking about?"

"My plane led her right to Secure One." Cal stuck a finger in his chest. "If she hadn't tagged my plane, you'd still be safe!"

Marlise shook her head while she tried to understand what he was saying. "No," she said without breaking eye contact. "You and your plane saved my life, Cal. I'd be dead if you hadn't come for me when you did. You had no choice but to use the plane."

"I could have gotten you out in an ambulance," he insisted, his gaze focused somewhere over her shoulder.

"Oh, you mean like the one Mack was driving when The Madame attacked? We could never outrun them in an ambulance." His grimace told her he knew it too. "The plane was the only option you had, even if it wasn't a good one."

"I made my business and home vulnerable to these people, and now we're paying the price. I will not lose you the way I lost Hannah."

"So what if she knows where you live? She doesn't have the manpower to attack it, or she wouldn't have tried to pinch me at the trial. Stop looking for any excuse to put distance between us, Cal. You played the hand you were dealt."

"And that hand put us right back in danger."

"Why are you so hung up on the idea that The Miss tagged your plane? It doesn't matter other than knowing we can't use it right now. We knew if The

Miss came back into the mix, this would always be the result—us stopping her."

"I've let everyone down since you and Mina entered our lives two years ago. I didn't have enough time to plan efficiently, which led to too many missteps."

"In the end, you saved the day, Cal. We will again this time too."

He gently took her face in his hands and offered a tender caress of his thumb across her temple. "Maybe that's true, but I liked that kiss way too much for it to be good for either of us."

"I liked it too, Cal. It was my first kiss, and I'm glad I waited for you."

His head tipped slowly in confusion, and he blinked once. "You've never been kissed before?"

She pinned her gaze to the carpet and shook her head. "No, I never allowed it. I wanted to save something for a man who might someday love me despite everything else I've been through."

"Marlise," he whispered, pulling her head down to his until their foreheads touched. "Not despite everything but because of everything you've been through."

"What did you see in me that day on the plane, Cal? I was a shell of a woman who was battered, broken and burned. You risked your life and the lives of your team for someone with little hope for a future."

"I didn't see the shell of a woman who was battered, broken and burned. I saw the woman you would become with a little care, love and respect from people who wanted nothing from you. People who wanted to help you heal from your physical scars and help you live with the emotional ones. That day on the plane, when we locked eyes, I saw the woman who ran through the woods for hours without complaint, all while bleeding. I saw the woman who would help put away a woman hell-bent on mistreating women like herself. I saw the woman sitting before me right now."

"You're just saying that to be nice," she whispered, wishing she could take his lips again and make him forget about everything around them.

"I don't say things just to be nice, Marlise. You know that. If I didn't trust my instincts, you wouldn't be here right now. You'd still be at Secure One if I didn't believe that you had the courage and guts to walk back into Red Rye and revisit your past."

"I even surprised myself," she said with a smile. "But I'm terrified of what will happen when the phones come on, and I have to see the face of the woman who tried to kill me."

"Use that fear," he said, moving his jaw forward and kissing her lips once before speaking again. "Put her image front and center in your mind and keep her there. Remember all the things she did to you and is still doing to other women. Use that fear and anger to help me find her and put her away for good."

"You believe I can, don't you?"

"I always have. I just need you to believe it too."

Marlise stared into his eyes, noticing they were the deepest, darkest brown they'd ever been since she'd been part of Cal's world. Was she the woman he believed her to be?

"You're right," she whispered, her breath held tight in her chest. "I've already done so many things I thought were impossible two years ago. If I could do those things, I can do this. I can help you find her and save the other girls."

"That's my girl," he whispered, his lips dangerously close to hers. "Are you ready to do that now? The phones should be ready to start up."

"I'm ready," she promised, taking his warm face in her tiny hands. She wasn't ready. She didn't want to break the connection they'd found here tonight, but she knew what her reality was, and it wasn't having Cal Newfellow once this case was closed.

"Before we do, I have to ask you something."

"Anything," she promised.

"Would it be okay if I kissed you again? When my lips are on yours, I forget all the responsibilities I face and the heartbreak I've suffered."

"No," she whispered and noticed the light dim in his eyes. "This time, I would like to kiss you because you do the same for me."

There were no more words then, just the sensation of floating in a different plane of existence while Cal teased her lips and showed her, rather than told her, how beautiful she was to him. When the kiss ended, they were both breathing heavily, and they took a moment to catch their breath.

"I know we have a lot to unpack with those kisses," she said, tucking her hair behind her ears. "But they gave me the strength and the courage to face The Miss again, and I don't want that feeling to disappear yet."

He let his hand slip across her face on his way to the desk. "Whatever makes this the easiest for you," he said, unplugging a phone and holding down the power button. She heard the *whoosh* when it came on, and she sat up straighter, strapping on her armor to prepare for battle. "I'll show you this, and then we'll call Roman and Mina and track this woman down. Are you with me?"

She took the phone from his hand and opened the gallery, taking a deep breath before letting her gaze flick to his. "This one's for Emelia and Bethany," she said right before hitting the hidden folder and accessing it with the password. A face filled the screen that usually only filled her nightmares. Not anymore. The Miss was real again. "You're going down," she whispered, right before she turned the phone for Cal to see.

Chapter Twelve

While Marlise processed the image on the screen, Cal took a step back and ran his hand through his hair. He was still reeling from the kisses they'd shared. He tried to conjure up an image of Hannah to clear his head, but he couldn't. His mind wouldn't show him anything but the woman he'd just kissed breathless. It had been thirteen years since he'd been remotely interested in a woman beyond a one-night stand, and then along came this little slip of a thing who ripped the carpet out from under him.

You have a job to do.

He did, and letting Marlise cloud his mind and steal his focus wouldn't get the job done. Resolving not to kiss her again was impossible, but he could flip into his mercenary mode and stay on a singular path. Find The Miss.

That little voice in his head laughed.

That worried him. He had to put Mary out of his mind, or she might end up in his heart. That was an excellent way to get them both killed.

"That's her," she said, rotating the phone for him to see. Staring back at him was a woman who could be anyone's sister, cousin or girlfriend.

"She looks so…"

"Normal?" Marlise asked, and he nodded.

"Look at her eyes."

Cal brought the phone to his face and concentrated on the woman. "They're hollow."

"As is her soul," Marlise agreed. "She won't stop until someone makes her."

"Then let's make her," he said, handing her the phone back and turning on the tablet he had set up to connect them to Secure One. He dropped his boss mask down over his face to hide the man who'd had his lips on a beautiful woman just moments ago.

"Secure two, Romeo," a voice said over the tablet.

"Secure one, Charlie."

The screen came on and Mina and Roman were squashed together to get into the camera. "So good to see you both!" Mina exclaimed. "Are you safe?"

"For now," Cal answered, motioning Marlise over to sit by him at the desk. "We had dinner and then fired up the phones."

"Did you find the image?" Roman asked.

"Yes," Marlise whispered after she sat. "Mina, I want to spare you from seeing her again, but you should confirm her identity."

Cal noticed Mina's lips purse as Roman put his arm around her. "You don't need to spare me, Marlise. I'm in it to win it with you. Show me."

Marlise turned the phone, and Mina's eyes closed for a moment, and she swallowed before she spoke. "That's her. That's The Miss. She looks so innocent, as though she could be an accountant or a teacher. But she's diabolical."

Roman leaned in closer to get a good look at the picture. "I saw her once from a distance in Red Rye. I didn't know it was her until after the fact. On closer inspection of that image, I wonder if she's a different nationality?"

"I always thought she was Latina," Mina answered.

"She did speak a lot of Spanish on the phone," Marlise pointed out.

Cal lifted a brow. "What did she say?"

"I don't know. I don't speak Spanish."

"I do," Roman and Mina said in unison.

"I never heard her speak Spanish," Mina added, "but I couldn't snoop the way Marlise could."

"She has no soul," Cal told his brother. "We have to find this woman before more women die."

"How's Charlotte?" Marlise quietly asked.

"She's okay," Mina said. "I'm checking on her often, but Selina is with her at all times. Mack and Eric are trading off guarding the med bay. I think she'd be more comfortable in a room though. She doesn't need the med bay anymore."

"Put her in my room," Marlise said immediately, but Cal shook his head.

"No, that's not a good idea. Keep Charlotte in the med bay until we get back, but put a better bed in there if you need to. Have one of the guys do it. I want eyes on her at all times."

"Cal, she's not working for The Miss," Marlise insisted.

"Maybe not, but I'm not risking it. I want her with someone at all times."

"Understood," Mina said.

It was Roman who spoke next. "Have you listened to the recordings?"

"Not yet," Cal answered, glancing at Marlise. "We just got in, showered and had dinner."

"Get me a recording of her voice and that image as soon as possible," Roman said. "I'll start voice and face recognition with them, but I doubt that will reveal much."

"I'll do that," Cal said. "Then we'll listen to the recordings and make lists of names, cities and any women she might mention. We need to find her quickly, so we have to be efficient."

"Agreed," Roman said with a head nod. "As soon as you have something, send it. We'll run it down while you keep listening."

"I may have gotten her on the recordings speaking Spanish," Marlise said. Cal turned and noticed it was as though she were talking to herself.

Cal's glance at the camera showed Roman and Mina were just as surprised as he was. "But you don't know who she was talking to?"

"No, but I remember a couple of times the phone was running when I was cleaning because her door was cracked. It always frustrated me when she spoke Spanish because I didn't know what she said."

"If you come across any Spanish recordings," Mina said, "send it over immediately, and we'll translate it."

"It may not matter," Marlise said, her shoulders heavy from fatigue and frustration.

Cal put his arm around her to give her a comforting squeeze. "Maybe not, but all we need is a name that we can trace, and her web starts to fall apart."

"That's our plan of action then," Roman said. "And you need to stay put until we have more to go on. I don't want you driving back here until we know you don't need to chase down a lead closer to Kansas."

"Understood," Cal said. "We'll listen to the recordings and then get some rest while you're reviewing anything we find. My hands are tied here, so I'm counting on you, brother."

"We're a team—remote or in person. We'll get the job done."

Roman and Mina signed off, and Cal turned to Marlise. "Ready?"

"As I'll ever be," she said, but he could tell she was lying.

"Why don't you rest while I start listening? You're ready to collapse."

Her shoulders squared before she spoke, and he bit back a smile. She wasn't going to rest. "I passed exhaustion about six hours ago. I won't lose sight of why we're here. I can rest when we've sent the information to Roman."

"But…"

Her brow lowered, and it stopped him in his tracks. "No buts. Here's the thing, Cal. You can listen *to* the recordings, but you don't know what you're listening *for*. I do."

"Fair point," he had to agree.

"There are only a few hours of recordings, so let's just get at it. The sooner we finish, the faster we find The Miss, get her into custody and free all the girls she's torturing."

He tapped the desk with a grin and pulled the phones and two notepads over to them. He pushed one at her and handed her a pen. "Ready?" On her nod, he opened the first phone, and they settled in. They needed to find one needle in the haystack, and once they did, he'd make The Miss wish she'd forgotten Marlise existed.

MARLISE WOKE SLOWLY, her gaze sweeping an unfamiliar wall. Where was she? It took her a few minutes to remember she was in a hotel with Cal. Their late night filtered through her sleepiness and she remembered they'd stayed up until 3:00 a.m. listening to the recordings. Cal was still messaging Roman when she went to bed, but she couldn't keep her eyes open a moment longer. She was just going to close her eyes for a few minutes, but now the sun was up. She couldn't help but wonder what Roman and Cal had found after she went to bed.

She tugged the blanket up to her chin, but met resistance halfway there. When her brain sorted out the incoming messages, she glanced over her shoulder. A man, giant really, had his nose buried in her hair as he slept. He had his arms wrapped around her, and when she tried to squirm out of them, he pulled her in closer.

"Just a little bit longer," he whispered, his warm breath raising goose bumps on her neck. "If we get up, we have to face bad guys again."

"You mean bad gals?" Marlise asked with a chuckle.

"Them too. I need a few more minutes to hold you and remember the good in the world."

Marlise leaned back and gave him the time he needed. She understood how he felt. No one wanted The Miss found and neutralized more than she did. More than Charlotte did. More than all the girls still under her thumb did. It was up to them to do it. They were the only ones with the means and skills to find her and make her pay. In fairness, she had no skills. Cal had skills. Marlise had knowledge, but knowledge could be a powerful thing.

She rolled over to face the man behind her. They were both dressed, and she noticed his gun on the nightstand next to him. "What happened to sleeping in shifts?"

"I couldn't wake you," he mumbled, but his eyes finally came open and blinked a few times. "I didn't think you'd mind as long as I stayed on top of the covers."

"I wouldn't have minded if you were under the covers. You're like a furnace, and I'm always cold."

"Is that your way of saying you trust me?" he asked, tracing his finger down the scarred flesh on her cheek. She didn't know why she allowed him to do it, but she'd probably make him stop if she ever figured it out.

"I guess it is," she agreed with a soft smile. "The last person I trusted nearly got killed though, Cal. Being around me isn't good for your health."

"No," he said, resting his finger against her lips. "Mina nearly got killed because of The Madame, not you."

"The common denominator then and now is still me, Cal."

"Again, no," he insisted. "The common denominator is evilness and greed. You talk about wars. Well, we're fighting one against evil and greed right now. We're in this together, and it will stay that way. Got it?"

Marlise had no choice but to agree. She knew he'd come up with rebuttals for any argument she made. Her battered heart had to admit that she liked being in this together with him. "Got it. Did you and Roman discover anything after I went to bed?"

"That's a negative. Roman's running her voice through voice recognition and putting her picture into the facial recognition program, but I doubt that will get us any hits since we know she was scrubbed.

Mina and Roman are translating the Spanish conversations this morning and will get back to us."

"Listening to those recordings again was difficult," she admitted. She couldn't admit it last night, but the intimacy of this moment made it easier for her to be vulnerable. "I let myself forget some of the terrible things that went on there. When I heard Bethany and Emelia, my heart broke."

"Hey," he said, wiping away a tear from her cheek. "It's okay to feel that way. What you went through in Red Rye was traumatic, and facing it again is like digging it all up after you just buried it."

"Yes," she breathed out. "So much. I knew we had to, but I didn't want to battle it again."

"But you did. That's what makes you a warrior. You faced a demon from your past, and by doing that, she no longer holds any power over you. I could only hope to be that strong one day."

"You are that strong, Cal. One day should be now. Stop living your life like you're already dead. You're not. You're the backbone of a team that relies on you and looks up to you. You're their leader. Be that leader, Cal. Lead by example."

"I wish I had the belief in myself that you have in me, Mary. I mean, Marlise. I'm sorry."

She rested her finger on his lips. "I don't mind it when you call me Mary. I just don't want everyone to."

"But you said you didn't like that girl."

Her words from last night came back to her, and she realized she'd confused him. She had to explain it in a way that made sense to him. "If I ask everyone to call me Mary, I worry I might become that girl again."

"But you don't mind if I use it?"

"You use it softly. When you call me Mary, there's a layer of understanding there. It's solidarity between warriors. It's an understanding between two souls who have suffered through the same atrocities in battle. You say the name with reverence, and that makes me feel..." She paused and met his gaze, unsure what the right words were. "Cared about as a human being. When you call me Mary, I feel like I deserve to be cared about, and I'm not a lost cause."

"Oh, sweet Mary," he whispered, his eyes revealing his emotions better than his words. "You deserve so much more than caring. You deserve love, happiness and joy in this life. You are not and never were a lost cause, baby."

Before she could say another word, his lips were on hers. It wasn't a hurried kiss of passion, but a tender kiss of caring. Even his gentle kisses raised her blood pressure and made her heart tap faster in her chest. He'd called her baby again. Whether it was consciously or unconsciously, she didn't know, but she would store it away in her heart for when he was no longer part of her life. And there would be a day when he let her go. Especially if he couldn't find a way to let go of the past.

Chapter Thirteen

He ran his fingers through her hair, his lips still on hers in a kiss that went from tender to passionate with one flick of his tongue. Cal leaned over, pinning her head to the pillow as a moan left his throat to fill her mouth. She fought to control the kiss just as a device across the room started buzzing, and Cal groaned. "That will be Roman."

"You'd better get it."

Cal climbed from the bed, and the loss of his heat was palpable. Feeling so bereft quickly scared her more than facing down The Miss.

Cal finally hit the button to end the buzzing.

"Secure two, Whiskey." It was Mina's voice this time.

"Secure one, Charlie."

The team all had code names from the alphabet that matched the first letter of their name. Roman was Romeo, and Mina was Whiskey since her real name was Wilhelmina. They opened any communication with their code phrase, so if the person on the other end was compromised, they didn't put the entire team at risk.

"Did I wake you?" Mina asked when the camera flipped on.

"Just woke up," Cal said, and Marlise noticed him subconsciously straighten his T-shirt. Everyone looked to him when they needed guidance and reassurance, and the way he switched into work mode in the blink of an eye meant he knew it too. He just needed to own it.

"I may have found something," Mina said without further preamble.

Marlise was off the bed and standing behind Cal immediately. "Did we get a hit on her picture?"

"No. We got a hit on the conversation you recorded in Spanish."

"Which one?"

"The long one that you risked your life to record. It was just before the fire. Your subconscious must have told you it was important. I translated the whole thing, but I'll give you the highlights."

Cal grabbed a pen and paper and waited for Mina to speak.

"She kept referring to the other person on the phone as *papá*, which means *dad* in Spanish."

"That's weird," Marlise said, joining them at the desk. "She always told us she was just like us and didn't have any family. That was her whole shtick about girl power."

Mina pointed at the camera. "That's why it caught

my attention so quickly. At first, I thought she was talking to a client. Sometimes they wanted to be called daddy."

Marlise and Mina simultaneously gagged and shuddered at the memory of those men.

"But that's not the case?" Cal asked, somehow knowing they both needed to be redirected.

"I don't think so." She picked up a piece of paper to read. "Everything is ready. I'm prepared to do what needs to be done to get out of this hellhole." Mina paused and then said, "That was loosely translated."

Cal and Marlise smirked at each other while Mina continued.

"My best girls are ready for the challenge. It's time to expose the agent. No, Dad, I'll take care of her myself. You don't need to come here. Stay far away from Red Rye, or this deal goes bad. You have taught me well, and I will not fail. This is our last contact until we reach the desert."

"The desert," Cal repeated, and Mina nodded.

"That was all she said about location, though Charlotte already confirmed they were living in a desert somewhere."

"A state that meets the border?" Cal asked.

"Honestly, it could be any of those, but we have a place to start. That narrows it down to Arizona, New Mexico and Texas. All about the same driving distance that Charlotte mentioned."

"Three states are a smaller hole to hunt than six,

but we need more," Cal said, tapping his finger on the desk.

Marlise stood up and started to pace. "The other conversation she had in Spanish didn't reveal any-thing?"

"No, but she was talking to the same person. That one was quick, but she said they'd hit the jackpot, and she had to move if they wanted to collect."

Marlise paused on her way past the screen. "Jackpot is a street name for fentanyl."

Mina tipped her head for a moment. "You're right. The conversation was so innocuous and rushed that I didn't link that when I listened. She was excited and talking fast, which made it harder for me to trans-late. I sent you the transcripts of both conversations. Read them over, and I'll do the same again. Call me when you're done."

The screen went dark, and Cal opened his en-crypted phone and handed it to her. "You read it and tell me if you can pick out anything. You lived with her. I didn't."

The short conversation wasn't as innocuous as Mina thought it was. "She also mentions Cactus, a street name for peyote, Red Rock meaning metha-done, and Beans meaning ecstasy. If she's referring to drugs, they're moving the hard stuff around."

"More likely her women were moving it."

"And when you move those kinds of drugs around, women disappear."

"Anything else?" Cal asked. Marlise knew he was

trying to keep her focus on The Miss and not the missing girls. Those girls didn't deserve what happened to them any more than she did, and Marlise would be the one to vindicate them.

"Well, we know her dad, whether he is her real father or someone else, was funding her time at Red Rye, and set her up in the new town, wherever that may be. They were using the women as drug mules in Red Rye, possibly with or without the knowledge of The Madame, and she piggybacked on The Madame's operation to build her own."

"But we still don't know where she is."

"Where's that list of cities we made last night?" she asked, handing him the phone and grabbing the pad he held out. She read off the cities to him. "Oklahoma City, Dallas, Fort Worth, Albuquerque and Phoenix were the cities where they did the most business. That matches up with the three states that sit on Mexico's border. If her 'dad' is south of the border, it would make sense she's in one of those states. I would pick someplace around Albuquerque."

"Tell me why," he said, ready to write on his notepad.

"It's the most centrally located to the other four cities. If The Miss is somewhere in New Mexico, her reach to the other cities is like a satellite," she explained, holding her arms out. "East or west, and she reaches one of the cities she used to send the Red Rye girls for dates. She probably kept those clients when The Madame went down because The Madame didn't know they were drug dealers. She was only seeing the escort side of the business."

"Possible," Cal agreed. "I'll call Mina back."

Once Mina and Roman were on the line, Marlise explained what she'd read and her thoughts on where The Miss could be.

"That's excellent linear thinking, Marlise," Roman said, bringing a smile to her face. "It's a place to start."

"Did Charlotte say anything more since we left?" Cal asked, clearly frustrated by their lack of progress.

"She's trying, Cal, but The Miss has them so isolated that she doesn't know much. Even when she flies them out, they're blindfolded until they're on the plane, and the plane has no windows. They fly into small airports, but it doesn't matter if the women know what city they're in by then because they're already away from home base."

"I'm going to be real with you, Mina. We may not be able to locate her. Secure One is good, but without a starting point, no one will find her. We may have no choice but to draw her out, capture her and then find the women."

Roman and Mina glanced at each other before they nodded. "That's what we were thinking too. Drawings of cacti don't help us find a madwoman."

"What?" Marlise asked, leaning on the desk to stare intently at the two people on the screen. "Drawings of cacti?"

"Yeah," Mina said, leaning out of the camera angle for a moment. "Charlotte is trying to help by drawing pictures of what she was able to see around home base." Mina held up a pad of paper with a pencil drawing. "It's like pods that stem off the main house."

Marlise studied the image Charlotte had drawn. It was surprisingly intricate and was easy to picture sitting in the middle of the desert somewhere. The middle house was a large camping trailer, and sitting at angles like sunrays were smaller ones.

"She told us that each of the smaller pods," Mina said, pointing at Charlotte's rounded campers she had colored silver, "house two women."

Marlise counted quickly. "There are fourteen pods."

"Which gives us a good idea of how many women are working for her," Roman said. "But that still doesn't matter if we can't figure out where this pod group sits."

"Wait, what's that?" Marlise asked, pointing at a drawing at the back of the image.

"One of the cacti she drew," Mina said. "I have a better image. Hang on." She shuffled through some papers and then held up another drawing. "Charlotte is an amazing artist," Mina said. "She helped us with several things we needed laid out here, Cal."

Marlise registered Cal's nod, but her focus was on the paper that held images of several different but intricate cacti. "That one!" she exclaimed, pointing at the paper on the screen.

Mina turned it around. "What one?"

"The big one. It's a saguaro cactus."

"A what now?" Cal asked, turning to her.

"A saguaro cactus. The kind you see in old movies that look like trees. They're tall and have arms that come up like branches," Marlise explained excitedly.

"We're on the same page," Cal said calmly and with great patience. "Why does that one stand out in your mind?"

"They only grow in one place in the country! The Sonoran Desert."

"How do you know this?" Roman asked, leaning into the camera.

"I'm from Arizona, Roman! It's one of the first facts you learn about your home state. If you see a movie with a saguaro cactus, you know it was filmed in the Sonoran Desert. Charlotte said it's scorching where they are, and the Sonoran Desert is the hottest one in both Mexico and the United States."

"You're saying that The Miss is hiding somewhere in Arizona?"

"Not just somewhere, Roman. The Sonoran Desert is less than two hours from the Mexican border."

"You don't think she crossed the border and is in Mexico?"

Marlise shook her head almost immediately. "Not with the girls. She'd have to have passports if she tried to enter legally or a safe route to travel by foot across the border, and those don't exist. If she had gone by herself, I would say it's possible, but not if she has that many girls. She stayed on this side of the border to run drugs. Not a question in my mind.

Mina, would you pull up an image of a saguaro cactus and run it down to Charlotte? Ask her if that's the one she intended in the drawing. We'll wait."

Mina nodded and took off, leaving Roman to stare into the camera. "I'm impressed, Marlise." His tone said he was genuine. "That was some great deducting skills. All we saw in those drawings was too much ground to cover."

"This is still a lot of ground to cover. The Sonoran Desert extends into California and down into Baja, but I know The Miss. She never took a girl any further west than Phoenix. She's in Arizona."

"How big is the desert in Arizona, mileage-wise?" Cal asked. "Do you know?"

"It extends above Phoenix to the north, the border on the west and about Tucson to the east," she said without hesitation. "It's still a lot of ground to cover, but I would concentrate on the area near the southern border. If she's running drugs and they're coming from someone in Mexico, she would want to be close. Hell, she might even cross the border legally with a passport and bring the drugs back herself."

Roman raised a brow. "I have some friends south of the border. I'll get the image to them and see what they know. It's risky on her part to use a passport, but we still have to check on the off chance she did."

Mina came back into the room and plopped down in the chair. She must have sprinted to get to the med bay and back that quickly. "Charlotte said yes. Those are the cacti she saw around their camp."

"I cannot believe that a woman with no law enforcement training managed to home in on a woman hell-bent on being a ghost with nothing more than a picture of a cactus. Mary, I'm in awe," Cal said, wearing a grin. He wasn't kidding around. She'd impressed him, and her heart soared.

With her head held high and her shoulders back, she smiled too. She suspected the feeling she had inside her chest was pride. "I want this to end so you can all be free again. Until we find her, we can't even rid ourselves of The Madame."

"What is the news on the trial?" Cal asked Roman, who was still on the screen.

"The trial is on hold. The defense is working hard to convince the judge they need to move forward, but so far, they've failed. The judge put everything on hold for two weeks. She has sequestered the jury but allows family visits in the hotel while supervised. At the end of the two weeks, I suspect the trial will go on, with or without Marlise."

"We have ten days left of those two weeks?" Cal asked, and Mina nodded. "Then we'd better get a plan in place and execute it before we run out of time. We've been here too long and need to get out of this town before bad characters stop by and hurt innocent people. I'm giving Mary point on this one. Are you guys in agreement?"

"Me?" Marlise asked in shock. "Why are you giving me point?"

"Isn't it obvious? Thus far, you've been the one to

find all the little crumbs The Miss didn't know she dropped. You know her and her habits. I'm putting my bets on you being the one to locate her and bring her down."

"I am too," Mina said with a wink.

Chapter Fourteen

The plane was in descent, and Cal was on high alert. They'd made it out of Kansas on a commercial flight to Phoenix, but that didn't mean they'd make it out of the Phoenix airport without picking up a tail. If The Miss was in Arizona, as Mary suspected, they would have to watch their backs until they secured her location.

"Are you sure this is safe?" she asked from the seat next to him. "I'm worried about Mina and Roman."

"They'll be fine," he assured her, holding her hand on his lap. "The Miss hasn't tried attacking Secure One since she sent her team in to scout it."

"That part is weird," she agreed with a head nod. "Why wouldn't she strike if she knew I was there?"

"Because she doesn't know you're there," he said immediately. "She doesn't know that we went back there after the failed attack at the courthouse. Since her women couldn't confirm you were at Secure One, attacking would be wasted resources without confirmation you're there. We also have to consider that she doesn't have a team big enough to attack a compound far from her camp."

"I wondered about that too," she whispered. "I figured she'd have a team watching Secure One at the very least. That's why I'm worried about Roman and Mina."

"That was a chance we had to take. We're running out of time, and driving to Phoenix was time we didn't have to give. We'll meet up with them at the hotel and make a plan in person. We need the backup they afford us, and we all work well together."

Her nervousness was making his belly skitter. Risking his brother's life wasn't high on his list of favorite things to do, but if Roman and Mina weren't with them, they didn't stand a chance against The Miss. His brother was smart, and his wife was brilliant, so Cal was confident they'd make it to Phoenix safely and without extra company. Then again, if Roman brought company with him unexpectedly, it could work to their advantage. They needed to find the woman, and following the fox back to her hole was an easy way to hunt. He wasn't going to tell Marlise that. She didn't need to worry more than she already was.

"I hate to even say this, but would it be such a bad thing if The Miss was watching Secure One? We will have to make contact with her somehow. If she followed us here, that would make it easier."

How does she always know what I'm thinking?

"Let's worry about getting out of the airport to

start with, okay?" he whispered as the wheels touched the tarmac. "Remember, head down, follow my lead and don't let go of me at any time."

He stood and gathered their backpacks from the overhead compartment, then helped her up to stand in line. He'd have to stop and pick up his checked luggage, which contained nothing but his firearms and electronics, but he couldn't risk leaving them behind. He might need both sooner rather than later if The Miss was waiting for them.

The trip through the airport was quick, and when he tossed the backpacks into their rental and climbed in, he refused to breathe a sigh of relief. They weren't out of the woods by any means. Anything could happen once they got on the road.

"Buckle up," he said, securing his own seat belt and ensuring hers was set up for her height. "The hotel is only ten minutes away, but anything can happen in ten minutes." He handed her his firearm. "You're on guard duty. Shoot first and ask questions later."

She glanced down at the gun and then to his face. "I've got your back, Cal."

He nodded once and started the car, but he couldn't keep the smile off his lips when he backed out of the lot and hit the highway. They had a date with destiny, and in his opinion, the sooner, the better, before he did something with this woman he couldn't take back.

MARLISE PACED THE hotel room floor, wishing it was bigger than a cardboard box. That wasn't fair; the room was decent sized, but Cal's presence made it feel smaller than it was. She was also trying to keep her focus off the one bed in the middle of the room. Once again, he'd gotten a room with a giant king-size bed covered in pillows and a plush comforter. It would be a great place if they were in the room for pleasure rather than business. Then again, Marlise wasn't sure Cal even knew what pleasure was anymore. He'd shut himself off from the world for so long that his life revolved around business and nothing else. Maybe she could change that one day, but today was not that day.

They'd gotten word that Roman and Mina had arrived in Phoenix and were on their way to the hotel. Cal was setting up a communications center with Secure One while they waited, but Marlise couldn't sit still. Phoenix was her hometown, and it brought back memories of Mary's life. The faces, names and pain the people in her past caused. The faceless people who had taken advantage of her, first as a child and then as a desperate young adult.

Hands grasped her shoulders, and she jumped at the intrusion to her memories. "Stop for a minute. Remember, there is no one left here who can hurt you. Once Roman and Mina get here, you have three layers of protection from anyone outside of these walls who want to hurt you."

She rested her head back against his strong shoulder and sighed. "How did you know that's what I was thinking?"

"Human nature. Phoenix is your hometown, and the memories will rise to the surface. Don't get sucked under by them. You're above all of that now. You fought against those old biases and now you're here to finish the job. You're here to win the gold against the people in your past who hurt you."

"That doesn't make me any better than them then," Marlise said with a shake of her head.

He turned her to face him and held her close. "That's where you're wrong. You will finish the job by standing on the moral high ground they couldn't find if it were right before them."

"Good prevailing over evil?" she asked, and his head tipped in slight agreement.

"If you want to put it that way, sure. You're in the right, they're in the wrong, and that's all there is to it. We're one step closer to bringing this woman in and handing her over to stand trial with her old boss. I look forward to your day in court because you will annihilate their defense and show the world who they are."

"You sure have a lot of faith in me, Cal," she said with a shake of her head. "I hope I can live up to it."

"I have faith in what I know, and I know you. I've known you were the one who would put an end to this since the day you ran onto my plane with a broken arm, broken nose and fierce determination in your eyes when there should have been nothing but pain. We will follow your lead because you know her world. That will be the advantage she didn't account for when it came to this game of cat and mouse."

"I sure hope so," Marlise said, swallowing around the nervousness caught in her throat. She wanted to be the woman he saw in her, even though it scared her to death to be that woman. Facing The Miss again in any arena was terrifying, but doing it when she wasn't in shackles was downright deadly.

"I know so," he said, kissing her nose as he gazed down at her. "Deep breath in, and remember, your friends have your back."

"Are you a friend, Cal?" she asked, their foreheads still connected. "Sometimes, I don't know if you're a friend or someone who puts up with me."

Before she blinked, his lips took hers on a ride of passion and desire that involved more tongue than the last time. She was breathing heavy and was desperate for air but didn't want the kiss to end. His lips still on hers, he answered the question. "If I were putting up with you, would I kiss you like that?"

"No?" she asked against his lips, and he nipped at hers, making her squeak. She knew what he wanted, and she gave it to him. "No, you wouldn't."

"Damn right," Cal hissed before he attacked her lips again and showed her just how passionate he would be if he let himself go.

Chapter Fifteen

The knock on the door dragged a groan from Cal's lips as he ended the kiss. His breath sounded heavy as he stood in front of her, still gazing into her eyes. What she saw there was lust, fear and an emotion she couldn't name.

"That will be Roman," he said as he grabbed his gun and stood to the side of the door to check the peephole.

"Secure two, Romeo."

Marlise heard Roman's muffled voice just as Cal lowered the gun and opened the door. The moment Mina was inside the room, she had Marlise in her arms in a fierce hug.

"I'm so happy to see you again. I've been worried sick."

"No need," she promised her friend. "Cal always takes excellent care of me."

Mina smiled and turned to face the brothers, who had walked into the room after securing the door. "He does, but we both know The Miss is ruthless and will stop at nothing to shut you up. I'll be worried until the day she's behind bars."

"Or dead," Marlise said with a shrug of her shoulder. "Prison is good but dead is better. Is that a terrible thing to say?"

"From your position, absolutely not," Roman said. "If I needed more proof of how evil she truly is, Charlotte is example C. That poor girl. The Miss put a tracker meant for a car inside her with no regard for the damage or infection it could cause."

"Not to mention she's forcing them to be assassins and run drugs," Cal added.

"Then let's shut her down," Mina said. "Charlotte wanted to come, but Mack wouldn't allow it."

"Mack wouldn't allow it?" Cal asked on an eyebrow lift. "Why?"

Roman lifted his right back at him. "On the defense that she wasn't strong enough to run if need be. Selina agreed. She has an infection in her leg from the tracker. Selina is running IV antibiotics, and said it will clear, but she has to stay off it."

"Mack is keeping everything on track at Secure One, then? Do I need to reach out?"

Roman let out a bark of laughter, then crossed his arms over his chest while he grinned at his brother. "He's multitasking. It'll do him some good to concentrate on more than work for once."

"All of that said, or not said," Mina grunted on an eye roll, "Charlotte is ready to help with whatever she can from Secure One. She sketched the positions of the spotters on The Miss's compound with some realism worthy of a gallery show."

"Charlotte was an artist living on the streets before joining the Red Rye house," Marlise said. "She would tag buildings whenever she wanted three squares and a bed. When The Madame came calling, she told me that she signed on the dotted line to get her record wiped. Supposedly, they'd hired her to do graphic design for their new start-up company. She had no inkling that they were starting up an escort service."

"I'm sure none of the women The Madame trafficked thought that would be the case. You certainly didn't," Cal said, his voice softer than usual when he addressed her.

She worried that Mina and Roman picked up on it, but there was nothing she could do if they had. Cal was right. None of the girls knew they were selling their souls down the road for a chance at stability. The only one who knew that was The Miss, and it turned out she had ulterior motives.

"Marlise, where did The Madame troll for women when you lived here?" Roman asked, picking up a tablet off the bed. "Were there specific places she'd send scouts to hunt for women?"

A chill ran through Marlise at the memory of that time. Cal put his hands on her upper arms and kept them there. It was a reminder that he was there to take care of her, and he wouldn't let her get hurt again.

"The train station, bus station and YMCA. They

also rotated through the public parks with restrooms and shaded areas. Girls hung out at the parks where they had access to water and toilets. They're too smart to pick up girls from shelters, but they do troll the campgrounds. That's where they found me." A shiver went through her when she remembered that first interaction with a scout. If only she hadn't gone with her that day.

"That's still a lot of ground to cover," Cal said, squeezing her shoulders to offer comfort.

That was when she remembered if she hadn't gone with the scout that day, she wouldn't have these people in her life. Wishing for a redo in the past always changed the future. Even after suffering so much pain and trauma, she wanted this future with these people in it. She could only hope that was the case after The Miss was caught.

"I need to talk to Charlotte," Marlise said, grabbing Mina's hand. "Can we call her?"

"Tell us why first," Mina said calmly while her gaze flicked to Cal's.

"Tell us what you're thinking, Mary. We'll listen," Cal promised.

Marlise glanced between them all for a moment. "Well, it's important we know if she's sourcing girls from the bigger cities. If she is, that tells us her camp is somewhere closer to the center of the state than the border," Marlise pointed out. "But my gut tells me she's further south of Phoenix."

"How far is it from Phoenix to south of the border?" Roman asked, pecking around on his tablet, but Marlise could answer him faster than Google.

"It's two and a half hours, which doesn't sound like that long, but if you get a nervous girl in the car, two and a half hours is a long time for her to change her mind. The Madame always kept the commute down to an hour. She also had the scouts talk up all the pampering the girls would get when they arrived."

"How does that apply to calling Charlotte?" Cal asked, and Marlise turned to him, grasping the front of his shirt.

"She lived with those girls for at least a year, Cal. Chances are, she knows where they're from, at least the new girls The Miss brought in."

"She has a point," Roman said, but she waited for Cal to agree.

When he gave the nod, she did an internal fist pump. While Roman got Charlotte on the phone, she forced herself to stay calm. If her theory was correct, they were in the wrong place and had to move farther south if they had a hope of finding this woman before the trial resumed. It might be a shot in the dark, but you missed all the shots you didn't take, and honestly, they had no other shots.

"Marlise has a question for you, Charlotte," Roman said, snapping Marlise back to the conversation.

"I'm happy to answer it if I can," Charlotte said, and Roman motioned for Marlise to ask her question.

"Charlotte, did you get to talk to the new women that The Miss brought to camp?"

"Sure, just like in Red Rye, we lived together, and the new girls were scared and wanted to talk."

"Did any of them tell you where they were picked up?"

The other end of the line was silent, and Marlise was about to ask Roman if the call had dropped when Charlotte spoke. "I should have thought of that before Roman and Mina left," she said. They all heard the disappointment in her voice that she hadn't.

"Don't feel bad," Marlise said immediately to calm her. "You haven't felt the best since you got to Secure One, and I just thought of it myself. I'm hoping to plot a few of them on a map to give us a better idea of where to start the search."

"Give me five minutes? I need to think when I'm not on the spot."

"That's fine," Roman said. "Have Mack call us back or text us the information."

They ended the call and stared at each other with frustration until Cal spoke. "What if The Miss didn't get the women from Arizona?"

Marlise started to pace, but she shook her head while she did it. "I'm sure she did, at least in the beginning. She was setting up shop and didn't have the time or the scouts to extend her tentacles too far. I wouldn't be surprised if the first few girls she got were snatch-and-run homeless girls off the street."

"You're saying The Miss had to build her army fast?" Cal asked.

"Exactly," Mina agreed. "If she were running

drugs through Red Rye, she wouldn't want those clients to defect to a different supplier. We know she was prepared to leave, which means her home base was likely ready, but she still needed women to get it running."

"When Charlotte gets back to us, I want to plot the cities on a map. We'll find the center of all of them and start looking for The Miss's girls there."

"Needle in a haystack though," Cal said with frustration. "When the sun comes up tomorrow, we only have nine days until the trial resumes without us."

"If you'd rather, we can—" Marlise's sentence was cut off when the phone rang.

"I remembered six girls," Charlotte said, "but I don't know if these towns are in Arizona, California or Mexico."

"I think we can rule out Mexico," Marlise said immediately. "You didn't need passports to move around the country, right?"

"No," Charlotte agreed. "That's a good point. Then if we're talking about that desert you mentioned, these towns have to be in Arizona or California."

"I'm ready," Cal said, holding a sheet of paper to write them down.

Charlotte listed off three names, and Marlise stopped her. "Wait, Three Points and Sahuarita are near the San Xavier Indian Reservation. Were any of them Indigenous women?"

"That was the vibe I got," Charlotte said. "Do you know where these towns are?"

"The first three are south or west of Tucson. What are the other three?"

Charlotte listed them off, and Marlise bit her lip as she leaned over Cal's shoulder. "Those towns are all within driving distance of Tucson." If The Miss was taking girls from just one town or specific area, that meant she didn't have time to be picky about who she was taking.

"Thanks, Charlotte," Marlise said before Roman hung up with her.

"The Miss must be desperate if she's taking women all from one area," Mina said, mirroring Marlise's thoughts. "That could put her on police radar."

"Unlikely," Marlise said, sitting on the end of the bed. "She's still only going to source homeless girls. They're already lost girls, so no one will miss them unless they have a close friend on the street."

"True," Mina agreed, glancing at the two men. "It looks like we need to get to Tucson."

"That's less than two hours by car," Marlise said before anyone could ask.

"Once we're down there, do you know where to start looking?" Roman asked, his gaze holding Cal's.

The breath that Marlise blew out was long and frustrated. "That's the problem. There is so much area to consider there. You've got Catalina State Park, Santa Catalina Natural Area, the Catalina Foothills, Saguaro National Park and Tucson Mountain Park. Those are just the ones around Tucson. There are many other wilderness areas along that route going west."

"You're saying we have found the haystack, but it's big, and the needle is still small," Cal deduced.

"We only have nine days," Roman said. "We don't have time to search all those places on the off chance The Miss has sent a scout out."

Her three friends continued to toss around ideas on finding the needle, while Marlise considered something even more important—finding the eye of the needle. They had nine days, and that wasn't much time when the scouts spend at least a week grooming a girl before they take her back to meet The Miss. Maybe when she first arrived, The Miss wasn't grooming the girls out of time constraints, but by now, she'd surely be back to her usual tactics. She wasn't dumb, and she knew that taking too many girls from one area was bad for business. That made a person too memorable to the other girls on the street. The last thing The Miss wanted was for her scouts to be followed back to the base.

"I doubt she's even taking girls from Tucson anymore," Marlise said as a hush fell over the room. "She may not even be recruiting right now."

Mina pointed at her. "She's right. She could be sitting fine with women, other than losing Charlotte. With what happened at the trial, she could be laying low and waiting for that to pass."

"We're going to have to draw her out, and there's only one way to do that," Marlise said, sitting up straighter. "We let her know I'm in town."

"Absolutely not!" Cal bellowed before the words

were barely out of her mouth. "You aren't trained for that, and we don't have the backup!"

Mina grasped his arm to quiet him. "She's right, Cal. If we don't draw The Miss out, we'll still be trying to find her when the trial resumes."

"We'll drive around the whole damn desert looking for her pods before we risk Marlise's life again!"

"We don't have time, Cal!" Marlise exclaimed with frustration as she leapt to her feet. "Some of the roads west of Tucson are nothing but dirt and lead deep into the desert! We don't have time to find the needle. We have to find the eye, and then we have to thread it. If we don't, she will always haunt us. I'm tired of this cat and mouse game, and every minute we stand here safely, another girl could be dying. I have enough on my conscience. I don't need more deaths weighing heavy there."

"It's too dangerous," Cal ground out, his insistence loud and clear, but Marlise noticed an underlying layer of fear.

She walked to him and braced her hands on his chest, but he stepped back, putting that wall back up between them. "You can tag me. You'll know where I am at all times."

"Tagging you doesn't help if The Miss dispatches you on sight."

"She won't," Mina said. "She won't do that in public. She'd have to deal with a body if she did it anywhere other than home base, and Marlise is too well-known because of the trial. The authorities would know immediately that The Miss did it and she was in the area."

"She'd still be dead, Mina," he hissed. "I'm not taking that chance with her life."

"I'll go with her and be her backup."

"Forget it!" Roman exclaimed from the end of the bed, where he was sorting out information coming in from Secure One. "The FBI is already going to have a cow that I took their star witnesses out of town to find a madwoman. Imagine if they get kidnapped! No, this is a bad idea for both of you."

Mina's eye roll at her husband was powerful, and Marlise had to bite back a smile. "The FBI isn't going to say a thing if we catch The Miss for them, which is something they've been unable to do. Besides, they don't own us anymore."

"Even if I wanted to, which I don't," Cal emphasized, "there's no way to tag you without The Miss finding it when you get to her. The first thing she'll do is search you."

"I'll already be there, and you'll have the location," Marlise said logically. "After that, it doesn't matter."

"It matters if she kills you when she finds it."

"You could tag me instead," Mina said, tapping her prosthesis. "She can't take this."

Roman took Mina's face in his hands. "This is not your war to fight, Mina."

"But it is, Roman," she whispered, not backing

down. "The Miss took two years of my life and my leg from me. This is as much my fight as it is Marlise's."

"It's a moot point. The Miss isn't dumb. There's no way she would grab either of you. She'd know it was a trick," Cal said to shut the conversation down.

Marlise's excitement drained away, and she plopped onto the bed. Cal was right. They'd spent the last two years evading The Miss. There was no way she'd believe it wasn't a trap. There was no way she'd believe they'd just throw themselves out there and wait to get snatched. If they were going to get to The Miss, they would have to be subtle. They needed to be found without being obvious about it.

"I know what we have to do." Marlise stood and pointed at Mina. "We need to head to Tucson today, but I'll need you to make a stop. If I give you a list, can you obtain what's needed?"

"Of course," Mina replied. "What's your plan?"

"We know we can't go in dressed as ourselves, so we hit the streets as girls looking for a better life. We visit some parks, knock on some doors and make it known we want out of the street life. Disguised, no one will know who we are, which buys us time."

"No," Cal said, but Marlise spun on him and stuck her finger in his chest.

"Do not tell me no. You gave me point on this in Kansas, and you can't have it both ways, Cal Newfellow! You can't say you want to find The Miss but tie our hands at every turn!" Roman was biting his lip when she turned to face them. "Right?"

Roman shrugged. "I have to side with her on this one, little brother. You did give her point, and you said you trusted her instincts. We're running out of time, and her idea is valid and credible if we put safeguards in place before they go out."

"I'm going with you," Mina said, grabbing Marlise's hand. "We were a team in Red Rye, and we're an even better team now. We have each other's back, right?"

"Right, but Mina, you don't have to," Marlise said, her gaze flicking to Roman, but he didn't look as upset as Cal did. "I'd understand if you'd rather be part of the team monitoring my movements."

"I do have to," she said emphatically. "I want a piece of this woman as much as you do, and I will not let you go out there alone. You've been alone all your life, but not anymore. Secure One has you now, and you've proven yourself to all of us. Even Cal, despite his growling and teeth gnashing."

"Mina," he warned, his jaw pulsing. "Do not push me."

Mina strode up to him and looked him up and down. "Or what? Are you going to fire me? Fine, fire me. I'm still going out tomorrow on the streets of Tucson with Marlise to find this woman. You can get on board or stand in the corner and pout while we make a plan, but we're running out of time. We have no other option."

They stared each other down for long seconds before Cal's shoulders sank, and he shook his head.

"I know you're right, but I don't like it. I don't like it at all."

"Neither do I," Marlise said, stepping close to him so he could feel her heat and know she was there for him. "But I trust you, Roman, Mack and the team at Secure One. I trust that Mina will have my back and keep me safe. For someone who doesn't trust easily, that's saying a lot. You've all proven to me with actions rather than words that you're not letting anything happen to me. You only need to prove it one more time. The most important time."

Cal's brown eyes were wide and held the truth that he hadn't said. He was scared. He was scared for her but also of losing her. His nod relaxed her shoulders, and she gave him one back. The action was of respect for her and her choices, which filled her with pride.

"I will agree to this, but we don't leave for Tucson until morning. We need the rest of today to make a plan and get everyone at Secure One on it."

"Agreed," Mina and Roman said together.

"I can accept that," Marlise said. "It's only ninety minutes to Tucson, so we can still be on the streets by ten."

"If we agree, then let's get to work. I want to find this woman and bring her in so we can get on with our lives without her hanging over our heads."

As Cal, Roman and Mina set up a battle station in their hotel suite, Marlise couldn't help but wonder if the life he planned to get on with would include her, or if he wanted to find The Miss as a way to end his commitment to her. The determination she saw in his eyes told her he was committed to keeping her safe, but the fear she saw in them told her he was just as scared as she was about her role at Secure One once this was over. She suspected they were scared for different reasons, and Marlise hoped that if she came out of this mission in one piece, so did her heart.

Chapter Sixteen

The sun had gone down on them as they'd plotted and planned this mission to the last "what if," but Cal still wasn't comfortable sending Marlise into the field. She knew the streets, but they were always fluid, and she'd been gone for too many years. Roman wasn't any happier about sending Mina with her, but it was better than sending Marlise alone. They could watch each other's backs, and there were better tagging options for Mina than Marlise. They'd tag her prosthesis with a tracker in hopes if they did find The Miss, they wouldn't know she was an amputee. As long as she kept the prosthesis hidden, they could track them.

Roman wasn't going to get any sleep tonight either, and Cal took a bit of comfort in knowing he wasn't alone in his distaste for this mission. Neither of them dealt well with not being part of it. They'd rather be out there clearing the field than sitting on their hands in a car waiting for something to happen. They didn't have a choice this time. Their presence would be noticeable and only hamper the women as they worked the streets. He had to trust Mina and her skills as an FBI agent. He also had to trust Marlise and her skills as someone who'd once lived on the streets. The only part he liked about the plan was disguising them beyond recognition. If they didn't know it was her, the scouts would be more likely to take her to home base as a willing participant rather than a hostage. The women just had to get them onto the property, and Secure One would do the rest.

Mina had gone out and bought the supplies, and in six hours, they'd don their disguises and leave for Tucson. A vast pit opened in Cal's gut, and he grunted, wishing this hell were over and they were back at Secure One. Did he regret bringing Mina and Marlise to Secure One? No, not for one second. This case had cost him time, money and sleep, but he'd gained so much more than he'd lost. He had his brother working with him now, a sister who was also an excellent hacker, and a woman who could be more than an employee and friend if this were a different time and place.

She already is.

He grunted at that voice again. Thinking that way was going to get one of them killed. That voice hadn't listened to him since Marlise stepped foot on his plane two years ago. He fought against it, but it never relented, and it was always loud in his head when the room was quiet. Marlise had gone to bed an hour ago and left him to brood in the corner. He'd sleep there in the club chair, his feet up on the luggage rack, instead of climbing into that giant bed with her. Holding her as she slept would be a terrible idea just hours before he'd have to let her out of his protective grasp. They needed to close this case so he could get Marlise out of his mind and his lodge.

"Tell me what happened," Marlise whispered.

The room was dark, and Cal sighed, glad she couldn't see his facial expression at the request. "I can't, Mary."

"You mean you won't," she replied with disappointment.

"No, I can't. The mission was classified. I can't tell you what happened."

"You can tell me what happened without specifics, Cal. I only need to know what happened to you and Hannah."

"What happened to the meek woman who never said a word when she first came to Secure One?"

"You taught her to stop letting people walk all over her."

Cal snorted, and while he didn't mean for it to be, it was tinged with amusement. "I have to admit that even when you're in my face about something, I still like my feisty Mary to my meek one."

My? Stop. Get that out of your head right now, pal.

"Then stop putting up a wall between us like you don't care."

Cal stood from where he sat near the window and walked to the bed. He lowered himself to the edge of it. "I do care, Mary, and that's why I put the wall up. Doing anything else could get you killed."

"I'm not Hannah, Cal, and it's time you stop treating me that way."

"I'm treating you the same way I would any other witness I had to protect."

"Good sell, but I'm not buying. Tell me what happened."

Why was he even considering her request? He hadn't told anyone what happened since the debriefing the week after the mission. He'd been in a hospital bed, a bullet wound in his chest, but his heart shattered to smithereens.

"We were young and in love. Hannah was, um—" Cal glanced at the ceiling "—on the same team. I'm not purposely being vague, but I have to be careful what I say."

Marlise took his right hand and started to massage his palm below his missing fingers. He wanted to draw his hand away and force her to stop, but her touch calmed the burning nerves. He knew she lived with the same kind of pain and wondered if she knew he suffered too. He tried to hide his discomfort from his team, and the prosthesis helped by protecting the sensitive digits, but he spent a lot of time pretending he was fine when he wasn't.

"I understand. Keep going," she said, her fingers massaging away the pain.

"She was specially trained as an interpreter as well. It was her job to go in and get the information we needed. It was my job to protect her while she did it. The big boss said to move in, but I wasn't comfortable with the lack of recon. When you're working with the government, you're never in control, and they told me the people we were looking for weren't active in our area. My limited recon said the same. We were both wrong. Hannah paid the price. That's the story."

Marlise sat up in bed and turned his hand over, rubbing her thumbs across the scars that crisscrossed it. "What happened, Cal?"

"I just told you!" he exclaimed, sending his hand into his hair on a deep breath.

"What you did was tell me something I already knew. You didn't do your job, and Hannah died. But what happened?"

"It doesn't matter, Mary!" he exploded, standing and walking to the end of the bed. His harsh tone didn't even make her flinch, and that worried him. If she was digging in, he had a problem.

"It does matter, Cal. Hannah mattered to you. You loved her, but you didn't get her killed."

"Yes, I did! I didn't see the rebel hiding in an abandoned building with a rifle! She was a duck in a carnival pond, and I stood there selling tickets!"

"Did Hannah know the risks when she went on the mission?"

"Of course, she did. She was part of the team and had the same training I did, except she was also a linguist."

"I'm not trying to be coldhearted here, but if she was trained and part of the team, she accepted that she might not walk out alive. You did the same thing. If I had to guess, you took a bullet that day too."

"You're wrong."

"I saw the scar, Cal. I may not be highly educated, but I lived on the streets, and I've seen things there. That scar on your chest? The doctors opened you up to get a bullet out of you. A bullet you more than likely took for her. Don't tell me you failed Hannah when you gave everything you had, including nearly giving your own life."

"Is it an option to get the meek Mary back?" Cal asked as he walked to the bed and sat on its edge again. "I'm not sure I like being challenged by this one."

She smiled, but she didn't back down, and that ratcheted up his heart rate until he felt a trickle of sweat down his back. If she didn't stop, he would do something they'd both regret, like take her as his own in this bed.

"Sorry, that woman is long gone. The Mary in front of you tonight has decided to accept the experiences that shaped her and made her the woman she is. You need to accept that what happened to Hannah all those years ago shaped who you are personally, professionally and emotionally. Stop locking up your emotions to avoid being vulnerable. We're all vulnerable, Cal. We all have an innate need to connect with another soul that feeds our own. Yes, you loved Hannah, but she's been gone for thirteen years. When will you start finding connections again that feed your soul?"

She slipped her tiny hand under his T-shirt and ran her finger down his scar. The sensation sent a shiver through him, and he grasped her hand to stop her caress. "That scar is why I don't make connections anymore, Mary."

"Is that why you covered the scar with a tattoo? To avoid being reminded of the one connection that was broken?"

"I covered the scar so I wasn't faced with my failure in the mirror every day. Is that what you wanted to hear? They cut me open to take the armor-piercing bullet from the muscle near my heart. A few millimeters were the difference between life and death for me. They may as well have cut my heart out the day they cut the bullet out. I haven't used it since, and I have no intention of letting that organ rule my head ever again."

Her laughter filled the silent room, and that damn organ inside his chest reacted to the sound with a thump against his chest wall.

"You're ridiculous. As though every decision you've made in the last two years hasn't been led by your heart."

"Don't call me ridiculous," he spat. "And you're wrong. I make decisions based on what's best for my business and nothing else."

"You helped Roman find Mina and then sheltered

them at Secure One. You risked your life and the lives of your men to get me out of St. Paul and then nursed me back to health while chasing down a madwoman. You flew your chopper to Minneapolis in the dark of night because your brother's soulmate was in danger, and you didn't even hesitate. You brought me back to Secure One and gave me a job when Mina batted her eyelashes at you. If you think that anyone believes you don't have a heart, you're dead wrong, Cal Newfellow. It's time you accept that organ has led you plenty the last few years, and it hasn't steered you wrong."

"The potential is there for it to steer me wrong to the point someone dies, Mary. I can't allow that to happen again."

"You can't stop it from happening again, Cal. Don't you see that?" she asked, her hands holding her temples in frustration. "There are people out there who act in ways beyond your control! You can mitigate the risk as much as possible, but you can't predict what someone else will do. Why can't you accept that?"

"Because if I accept that, I'm going to do something I regret! I'll lose someone I care about to something beyond my control again!" His exclamation came from across the room where he'd darted when confronted with the truth he always knew but refused to acknowledge.

She was standing in front of him now with her hand on his chest. "Let's be clear here," she whispered, her gaze holding all the truth she knew about this world. "That statement is coming from fear and not truth. You're afraid you'll lose someone else you care about to something beyond your control. You don't *know* that you will. That's the difference. Unfortunately, that's how life works, Cal. Tomorrow is never guaranteed. Telling yourself you don't care when you do isn't going to make it any easier when that person is gone. You've got to care about people and love them while they're here, or all you'll be left with is regrets."

His silence was the gulf between them, even as she stood inches away with her beautiful, youthful, innocent heart laid bare. The moonlight slipped through the curtains and rested across her face to illuminate the scarred flesh.

She grabbed his wrist when he slipped his hand up the webbed skin of her cheek. "Stop." He could tell she'd wanted it to be forceful, but all he heard was sadness. "Don't touch me there."

"Because?" His voice *was* forceful. He wanted an answer and demanded she give it.

"It's my Mr. Hyde side," she whispered. "I look like a monster, Cal. That's why I wear my hair over it. That way, no one is confronted with the truth of how The Miss abused me. Most especially you. I've been used and abused over and over again in this life, and I wear this skin as a badge of shame. I don't know why you want to touch me at all."

Cal's heart broke, each word splintering off pieces

of it until it lay shattered at his feet. His poor girl had suffered through so much at the hands of these people. The burns may be healed but those scars—the scars that were slashed into her memory—would remain open, weeping wounds until someone loved her enough to heal them.

"Sweet Mary," he whispered, trailing his hand up the left side of her face to her temple, where his thumb rubbed the skin to soothe her eye. "Your burns don't detract from your beauty. They add to it."

Her eye roll was strong in her right eye. "Nice try, Cal. I don't even have a real eyelid on the left. There's nothing beautiful about it."

"I'm sorry you feel that way, love," he said, gentleness in his tone. "Because I think it shows your strength and resiliency to live through an event meant to take you away from this world. It shows your determination to go on with life when you had every reason to call it a day. Your future after that fire was bleak at best, but you didn't care what the future held as long as you were part of it. You want to be here, and you have no qualms about risking your heart or your life to keep someone you love safe."

"I trust you, Cal," she whispered. "I trust you to take care of me and protect me. That's why I can take risks to help those I love. You're the first man I've ever trusted because my heart said you were safe. My heart is connected to yours. Whether you like it or not. Whether it's convenient or not, I can't decide for you. All I know is, when you're near me, I feel safe, even when bullets are flying. If I didn't trust you to keep me safe when we faced The Miss again, I wouldn't have left Secure One to testify. I wouldn't have followed you back to a place that tried to take my life and walked into it with my head held high. I would have been too scared, but you were with me and kept me safe."

I trust you, Cal.

Those four words were a jolt to his head and heart that he couldn't deny. He couldn't deny that everything this tiny scrap of a woman said made more sense than anything he'd told himself over the last thirteen years. Through her eyes, he could see that he'd built his life around getting a redo on that day in a land far away when he'd failed someone he was tasked to protect. Every time he kept a client safe or a mission went the right way, it was another piece of metal he added to his armor when he should have been removing it.

"You're so much braver than I am, Mary," he whispered, his forehead touching hers now. "Your heart leads you to the truth every time."

"It does, Cal," she whispered, her gaze flicking up to his. "You can be that brave too if you start listening to your heart instead of your head."

"My head protects me, Mary. It protects me from all of…this."

"This? Do you mean connecting with someone who wants you to be happy? This? As in having any emotion other than anger in your life? This? Like having to admit that losing Hannah was horrible and the hardest thing you've ever lived through? It wasn't your fault, and you did live through it, so why aren't you living?"

Cal didn't let her finish. His lips were on hers before the next word left them. She wrapped her arms around his neck and fell into him. His strong arm around her waist lifted her off the ground, and her soft mewling mixed with his tight moan as he carried her to the bed. Cal braced a knee on the mattress and lowered her to rest against the soft comforter as he followed her sweet lips down.

This is a bad idea. You'll love her and lose her just like the last time.

"No," she said against his lips, "this is not a bad idea."

How could she know that was his exact thought at that moment?

"I see you, Cal," she whispered. "You wear your self-doubt like armor, but it's invisible to me. The man you hide away is the only one I can see. The good, the bad and the ugly. Just the same as you with me."

"Be that as it may," he ground out, his need pressing against her in a way that betrayed his words, "that doesn't make this the right choice."

"That makes this the *only* choice," she whispered right before she trailed her hand down his taut belly to his hardness yearning for her touch.

The moan left his lips before he could stop it. He

didn't want to stop it. He didn't want to stop feeling this way. Her tiny, sweet hand had slipped inside his jeans and wrapped itself around him. He throbbed against the heat of her hand and the idea that she offered exoneration from his past. He hadn't allowed himself to believe that was even a possibility since that day when he took a bullet for the woman he loved, and it still wasn't enough.

"It was enough," she whispered, her warmth spreading through him as she held him. "You are enough, Cal. It's time to share our pain until it's diluted and insignificant to who we are together."

His lips attacked hers again and stemmed the flow of truth from them. The truth was, he had already lost the battle of not caring about another woman the moment she ran onto his plane. Tonight, as she stripped him bare of his clothes and his demons, he knew it. He knew it when she gripped him in her tiny hand and let her heat soak into him. He knew it when he kissed his way from her lips to her breasts and then to her center. She was everything he'd tried to forget existed. Sweetness. Honesty. Pureness unsullied by his poison. He wasn't poison though. Not to Mary. To Mary, he was salvation.

"I don't have any protection," he moaned against her belly when his senses returned for a moment.

He gazed into her eyes and saw the truth. She was his protection. Her tiny presence in his life had been what could shield him from the ugly all along.

"Let me protect you this time, Cal," she murmured.

He sank into her, accepting her as the final puzzle piece to his unhealed heart. His lips were on hers when he spoke. "Mary," he whispered on a moan of pleasure. "You make me whole. You are home."

She tipped her hips up and let him slide deeper to rest against her center. "I'm more than home, Cal. I'm redemption."

Chapter Seventeen

Cal didn't recognize Marlise when Mina had finished with her makeup. Her facial scars had been
covered, and she wore a disheveled wig along with
clothes that hung on her slight frame. An old, thread-
bare flannel shirt covered the burn scars on her arm,
and fingerless gloves kept the scars hidden on her
hand. The weather in Arizona had cooled now that it
was fall, so pants and a long-sleeved shirt wouldn't
raise suspicion on the street.

Mina had done much of the same to hide her identity. A pair of men's cargo pants made her prosthesis disappear inside the material and would raise no
suspicion. She had traded out her everyday leg for
her running blade inside a tennis shoe, just in case
they needed to abort the mission and run. Mina ran
around the compound every morning and was confident she could escape any situation. He was confident she could too. Regardless of how things went
down a few years ago, she was still a trained FBI
agent, and she kept her skills sharp. Marlise, on the

other hand, didn't have the skills or instinct that Mina did. He hoped she would default to Mina if she told her to run.

He groaned and rubbed his chest with his palm. He'd had heartburn since he woke up yesterday. Marlise's lips on his skin were the only thing that soothed it, but it was back in full force when she stopped. The women had spent the day yesterday pounding the pavement and trying to get noticed, but no one approached them. Once the sun went down, they walked back to a rent-by-the-hour motel. Cal and Roman did the same thing. Cal refused to allow them to sleep on the streets, but he also knew they couldn't all be seen together. He had traded off watching their room with Roman last night. This morning they'd given them a head start and followed in the van. They were down to eight days to find The Miss, and Cal had doubts this would work.

"How'd you sleep?" Roman asked from the seat next to him in the van. They were waiting in a park at the moment. They'd move around throughout the day, so they didn't attract suspicion, but they had to stay close to where the women were.

"Didn't get much sleep. Don't tell me you did knowing you had to send Mina back out to the wolves today."

"Mina has been my partner for years. Yes, she's my wife now, but I still trust her skills as an agent. She's going to take care of Marlise. No offense, but you're jumpier than a cat on a hot tin roof, and that's not the Cal Newfellow I know. What gives?"

"You realize that when someone says 'no offense,' it's obvious that whatever they're going to say is offensive, right?"

Roman's whistle was long and low as he shook his head at his brother. "Wow, your deflection game is strong this morning. What are you trying to hide?"

Cal refused to participate in his nonsense. He'd do his job and focus on keeping Marlise and Mina safe from a madwoman. The last thing he would do was tell his brother he'd slept with their witness. He would remember that night for the rest of his life. The power that little thing held over him was unyielding, and he didn't know what he was going to do about it. How was he going to let her go when this was over? He had to though. She deserved a chance to go out and live her life, but watching her walk out of his was going to gut him.

He kept his gaze trained on the empty grass in front of him, hoping for a glimpse of the woman he'd made love to three times the night before last. No. It wasn't making love. That was dangerous thinking. Seeing it as anything other than a one-night stand was a fast way to lose objectivity when it came to this case. He checked his earpiece, listening to Mina and Marlise talking with other women. They'd been asking questions about where to get a hot meal and a shower, but none of the other women were forthcoming.

"Come on, Mary," Mina said. "We'll go find the YMCA."

Cal and Roman knew that was her cue that they were moving. Within seconds their GPS device popped up with a route to the nearest YMCA. Mack was back at Secure One, blazing a path to save them time. Cal started the vehicle and followed the GPS to an abandoned house near the Y. He parked on the street, knowing the women would eventually walk past the van and they could get a glimpse of them.

"Have you told Marlise about Hannah?" Roman asked as he leaned against the door of the van.

"Why on earth would I tell her about Hannah?" Cal growled the question more than he spoke it. The last thing he wanted to do was engage in a conversation with his brother about his dead girlfriend. Roman had been there that day, and he knew too much.

"Fair is fair." Cal glanced at him with an eyebrow down, not understanding what he meant. His brother shrugged. "If she's going to compete with a ghost, you should at least have the decency to tell her."

"She's not competing against anyone, Roman."

His snicker made Cal want to punch him in the nose. He wasn't a violent man, but Roman never eased up on him about Hannah. It had been this way for years. Every time they saw each other, Roman was bugging him about letting Hannah go and forgiving himself for what had happened. Cal didn't know how. Every job he did, every person he saved, was a way to find redemption from the one time he had failed.

"Marlise is more astute than you give her credit for, Cal," Roman said, shaking his head. "If you think she doesn't have your number, you're dumber than you look."

"Roman?"

"Yeah, Cal?"

"Shut up."

"Not this time," Roman said with a shake of his head. Cal was worried their ongoing pact of telling each other to shut up when they didn't want to talk had ended. "Everyone on this team can see how you've looked at Marlise since we picked her up in St. Paul. When will you be honest with her? The moment before she walks out the doors of Secure One, or never?"

"She knows about Hannah," Cal said between clenched teeth. His gaze was pinned to the rearview mirror as he waited for them to approach. It took several minutes to realize Roman was silent. He had his mouth open when he glanced at him, staring out the windshield. "Don't be so dramatic."

"You have to forgive me for being dumbfounded. I never expected you to tell her."

"I tried to use Hannah as an excuse—"

"And our little Marlise called you on your crap, right?"

Cal's shrug said everything. It brought a grin to Roman's face. "They're approaching."

Roman turned his head to watch the side mirror while Cal kept his attention on the rearview mirror. He wanted to catch a glimpse of Marlise to make sure she was okay.

"It's unbelievable how brave she is to go back into this life," Cal said as the women walked by the van without taking notice. He knew they had, but they didn't let on.

"There's one thing I've learned about women, Cal, and it's simple. As men, we always underestimate them. We underestimate their strength, stamina, grit and how their moral compass guides them. After finding Mina a year after her injury, still trying to solve the case, I was never more aware of how much strength it took her to keep fighting when she had every right to give up. Marlise has all that strength and then some. At least she does now that you've taken care of her, built up her health and acknowledged her contributions to the company. You allowed her to lead, a job she's never had before, and that's why she's out there right now. She wants to contribute to solving this case and freeing herself from her past."

"We're on the same page there," Cal said as he watched them walk toward the doors of the YMCA. "I want her to be free of The Miss."

"But you're afraid that means she will walk away from you."

"From Secure One? Absolutely. She's an asset to our team, Roman."

His brother's snort was loud inside the van. "Sure, you're afraid you'll lose her as a team member of Secure One. I almost buy that, Cal. If you think we can't see something has changed between you two, you underestimate my skills as a special agent of the FBI."

"Leave it alone, Roman. We have one focus, and that's keeping our girls safe."

The goofy smile his brother wore on his face told Cal that he already suspected what had happened between him and Marlise, but he wasn't going to confirm it. His time with Marlise was too special to sully by acting like it meant nothing to him. He hadn't had time to process it all, but he knew it meant something to both of them. Cal regretted his decision not to be honest with her, and he hoped he could be before it was too late.

"Don't ask about showers here," Marlise said to Mina as they approached the doors. Roman glanced at Cal with a questioning look, and he shrugged. "If they say they're available, they'll expect us to use them. A shower is going to blow my cover."

"Good point," Mina agreed. "I should have thought of that."

Cal couldn't help it. He was grinning like the Cheshire cat. "That's my girl."

Roman punched him playfully, but all playfulness disappeared when another woman approached them. Cal flipped the record button on and shifted the audio from their ears to the computer. They both held their breath and hoped they weren't going to blow their cover this early in the game by having to rescue them before they found The Miss.

"Yo," Marlise said to the girl as she approached. "Is the Y open?"

The girl looked her up and down and then did the same with Mina. "Sure ain't."

"Damn," Mina huffed. "I guess there's no point in staying then, Mary. Let's hit it."

Both women turned back the way they came when the other girl spoke. "What ya looking for there?"

Marlise turned back slowly and took a moment to assess the woman in front of them. She wasn't a street girl. Her good hygiene and clean clothing made her stick out like a sore thumb in a place like the YMCA. She was a scout. She was also Latina. Marlise reminded herself she could be a scout for any sex trafficking ring and forced herself to remain calm. She slid her eyes to Mina, who had a brow raised in the air. She was going to leave it to her to feel out.

"We're tired of the street, you know? Looking for a place to get a meal and sleep for the night where we don't need to keep one eye open."

"I could find work again if I could get a shower and some clean clothes," Mina added. "We both could. She cooks, and I clean. We were hoping to find a hotel that was hiring."

"I might know a place," the girl said. Marlise noticed she was trying too hard to be casual. She was excited and nervous, two emotions Marlise knew well.

"You saving it for yourself?" Mina asked. "Respect, if you are. We're all out here scrapping."

"No, but I know the owners, and I don't recommend just anyone to them. I gotta trust them, you know."

Marlise held up her hands in the don't shoot position. "Understood, sister. No harm, no foul. We'll be on our way."

"Wait! I could take you over there, and you could maybe show them your skills?" the girl asked before they could turn away. "They might even give you a room for the night as payment."

"How far is the place?" Mina asked. "We've already walked five miles today."

"It's about forty-five minutes from here, but my car is just up the block. I'm Jen, by the way."

"I'm Mary, and she's Amy," Marlise said, hooking a thumb at Mina as she eyed Jen with suspicion. "What are you doing here if the hotel is forty-five minutes away?" She took a step back and widened her eyes, hoping she looked nervous and agitated. Mina did the same thing, and the girl took a step forward but waved her hands innocently in front of her.

"I was supposed to meet some other girl here who was looking for a job, but she's a no-show. I already told the owners I'd found them some help, and now I hate to go back and tell them otherwise. I saw you two coming and thought you'd be interested. If you're not, that's fine, but I gotta get on my way."

Mina held up her finger and pulled Marlise aside. She put on a show of bending her head to whisper as though they had to weigh their options. Their only option was to find out if this girl was one of The Miss's scouts. "Do we go with her?" Mina whispered near Marlise's ear. "No way to know if she's with The Miss or someone else."

Marlise held her gaze and raised her voice to a stage whisper so the other girl could hear. "We have to take any chance that gets us off the street, Amy. I'll do anything to sleep in a real bed again. Imagine not having to worry about men following us or sleeping in shifts. I know you want it just as much."

With a feigned eye roll, Mina finally nodded once. "I do, but we gotta be careful, you know. And we stick together. No matter what."

"No matter what," Marlise agreed, doing some goofy handshake thing they'd come up with as a way to tell Cal and Roman that they should follow at a distance. The guys could hear them, but Marlise didn't want to take any chances that the mic wasn't working. They needed the backup where they were going. She could feel it in her bones.

Chapter Eighteen

"I don't like them getting into a car," Roman said as he buckled his belt and waited for Cal to put the van into Drive.

"Me either, but we have to trust Mina. All we can do is follow them and be ready for any situation that comes at us. Sex trafficking is so common on the streets that you could walk into a ring on any corner. There's no way to know if this scout is one of The Miss's."

Once the women were out of sight, Cal shifted into gear and idled with his foot on the brake. The computer was up, and they were still recording their conversation as they walked up the road. Thus far, the conversation had remained innocuous about living on the streets and the problem with finding a job when you didn't have a permanent address. Mina and Marlise were spreading it on like peanut butter, and he hoped it wasn't too thick. If this girl was from a different ring, they didn't want their cover blown in town.

"The chances are slim this woman has anything to do with The Miss," Roman said as they waited.

"Maybe not, but we have to take any chance we get. We don't have time to be picky. I hate to sound ominous, but the hair on the back of my neck went up when the girl approached."

Roman's response was simple. "Mine too. I guess we'll know soon enough."

"This is a nice BMW," Mina said.

"Come on, my girl," Roman whispered, his pen against the paper as he waited.

"I've always wanted to ride in a Gran Coupe. The lines are sleek, and the silver paint makes it look like a bullet. I bet it's as fast as one too."

"How do you know so much about my car?" the scout asked suspiciously. Cal glanced at Roman with a grimace, but Roman held up his finger.

"My old man. He got this, like, car magazine, every month. He'd go on about the cars in it during dinner and how he would have one someday. He was a mechanic, so he loved cars, but also booze. The two don't mix, and he wrapped his not-so-fancy Chevy around a tree."

Roman did a fist pump and snickered as he eyed Cal.

"Tragic," the woman said with zero empathy in her voice.

"Not really. Daddy was mean when he drank, and he always drank. The only thing I miss about him was the little bit of support he gave me."

They counted three doors closing, and then the engine purred to life. There was a crinkling of bags, and then the woman spoke. "Here are some snacks. Help yourself while we drive so you aren't hungry when we get to the hotel."

"Thanks!" Marlise said, pouring on the gratitude so thick even Cal smiled. "We haven't eaten in a couple of days."

Cal and Roman listened to the crinkling of wrappers and their fake moaning as they ate whatever snacks the woman had given them. Roman had to hope none of it was laced.

"What do you do for a living?" Mina asked after five minutes.

Cal glanced at the GPS that showed they were headed west toward the California and Arizona border. "Contact Mack and ask him to check for any issues going west on 86."

"Too easy. This is too easy," Roman said with a shake of his head, but he flipped open the phone to call Mack.

"I'm starting to feel the same way," Cal agreed as he stayed out of the car's line of sight but followed the GPS tracker Mina had in her leg. "Maybe not though. The women were out yesterday. Word could have gotten around that they were looking for a job."

"Or one of The Miss's guards was a scout and recognized Marlise."

Roman said the words Cal was trying not to think. Cal didn't respond. He was already thinking ten steps ahead of where they were. If their ride ended at The Miss's camp, it would be up to the women to get that information to them. Once they knew the location, Mack would let the local authorities know in the closest town while Cal and Roman found a way onto the property to protect Marlise and Mina. His experience with The Miss told him it would never be that easy. She was paranoid and wouldn't risk bringing Marlise into the camp without knowing she wasn't being tailed.

Roman hung up the phone and pointed at the GPS. "He's putting in all the roads that branch off 86 up on the screen. I'll focus on the GPS tracker while you focus on making sure we don't get noticed."

Cal set his lips and eased off the gas pedal. He didn't want to spook this woman before they got where they were going. The element of surprise would be challenging to maintain, but if he didn't, he might never see Marlise alive again.

THEY'D BEEN DRIVING nearly an hour when Jen turned off the highway. "We're kind of far out in the sticks for a hotel," Mina said, making a show of looking out the windows on the side and the back. "Who stays way out here?"

"You'd be surprised how many men are looking to play cowboy in the desert. My friend's hotel is always booked."

A shiver ran through Marlise. She knew what kind of hotel Jen meant and wanted nothing to do with it.

Not after spending the night with Cal. Was that only two days ago? It felt like an eternity since he'd held her in his arms. She was determined to do anything to get back to him. She regretted not telling him her true feelings for him before they parted ways. If she didn't make it out of this, he'd never know how much he meant to her.

Her mind went to the way he'd made love to her that night, and she wondered if that was true. Maybe they'd used their bodies instead of their lips, but she'd told him how she felt. He would only have to think about how she loved him that night to know she would love him forever. She shook her head. He'd already lost one woman he'd cared about in this life. Marlise refused to do the same thing to him. She'd worked too hard to show him that life and love were worth taking a chance on again. It was time to put the fear aside and do anything she had to in order to get out of this alive.

"How many rooms are in the hotel?" Mina asked as they bounced over ruts and holes in the dirt road.

"It's a unique property. You'll see once we get there. The owner is very devoted to giving her guests the best desert experience possible. The hotel is in pods, and there is plenty of privacy for the guests."

Marlise glanced over when Mina tapped her knee against hers. Mina nodded. She believed they were headed to the right place. Mina crossed her fingers together, and Marlise understood. They had to stick together and not get separated. Anything else was a death sentence. Marlise's heart pounded with pent-up anxiety when Jen steered the BMW down a driveway and stopped at a gate. Two women dressed in black fatigues stepped out, and Jen put her window down.

Marlise glanced at Mina, who wore total disregard on her face. She turned away and looked out the window as though she didn't have a care in the world. Marlise realized why. The guards were the same two who'd helped The Miss in Red Rye. They were in the right place. The time had come to face the woman who had tried to do everything in her power to break them. She'd failed, and this time, Marlise would finish the job. She bent down as though she had dropped something on the floor and whispered the two words that would set her future in motion. "Red Rye."

CAL ALMOST MISSED the two words that came across the computer speakers. *Red Rye.* He glanced at Roman from where they sat along the side of the road.

"Did you hear that too?"

"Red Rye," he confirmed, and Cal's heart picked up its pace.

"It's go time, brother," Roman said, strapping on his bulletproof vest and then his tactical pack. They needed as much firepower as they could carry. If things went south before help arrived, they'd have to shoot their way in, and out, to get Marlise and Mina.

After alerting Mack, they slid from the van and took off on foot. The sagebrush offered them surprisingly good coverage as they worked their way past the road Jen had turned down, and they followed the GPS on their small tablet that took them along the west side of the property. They'd find cover and then wait for the trackers on the women to stop moving before they approached. They could still hear what was going on through their earpieces. For now. There was no guarantee that the link would remain once they brought Mina and Marlise onto the compound. The recording devices were hidden in a button on their clothing and undetectable to a wand, but that connection would be broken if they made them change clothes.

Cal slowed his breathing as they ate up the distance between them and the women they loved. The word tripped him up, and he went down to his hands and knees, a soft *oof* enough to turn Roman back to him. While he should be on the alert for an attack, he was worried about being in love. It was an inconvenient fact that he would have to face eventually. Now was not the time. Losing focus before they captured The Miss was a death sentence for all of them.

Roman pulled up inside a hoodoo that offered shade and cover from the sun beating down on their backs. "You okay?" Roman asked when Cal reached him.

"Tripped on some underbrush," Cal answered, taking a drink of water from his bottle. He noticed Roman smirking, but he refused to comment on it. "How far out are we?"

"Hard to tell. Two klicks or less from the western side of where they stopped. I've been listening, but it's been quiet, other than the sound of soft murmuring. I think Jen is talking to the guards about her new arrivals." Roman stopped and held up his finger as Mina's voice broke through their earpieces.

"Wow, that's a cool hotel!" she exclaimed.

Roman raised a brow at Cal. Obviously, they'd cleared security and made it onto the compound.

"It reminds me of a satellite or the sun," Marlise said enthusiastically. "I bet the kitchen is a fun place to work."

"Forget the kitchen," Mina said. "Imagine how cute those little pods are on the inside. I can't wait to start working."

Cal rolled his eyes, but he couldn't stop the smile from taking over his lips. It was no laughing matter, but he couldn't help it. "Spreading it on a little thick, aren't they," he said to Roman.

"Fastest way to The Miss is with a brown nose, and both women know that."

"They better slow down until we figure out a way to save them," Cal grunted while checking his equipment. "There are only two of us and an unknown count surrounding them. We don't stand a chance if we have to go in before the authorities get here."

"We need to move as close to the property as possible in case we have to go in. My wife will not be injured by this woman again."

Cal squeezed his brother's shoulder. "I'm hoping

they can buy us some time. If they're going to prove themselves to the boss, they'll have to work for a few hours, right?"

"We can hope," Roman said as their earpieces came to life again.

"This will be your pod while you're here," Jen said after the car doors slammed shut. "There are clothes on the beds, and you're welcome to shower and clean up. Once you've had a few minutes to rest, I'll take you to meet the owner."

"Already?" Marlise asked with fake nervousness. Then again, Cal wondered if it was fake. "Don't you want us to work a little bit to prove ourselves?"

"That's up to The Miss. She prefers to hand out the assignments each day. If we're short-staffed, it's my job to find new helpers."

A trickle of sweat ran down Cal's spine at the mention of her boss. They had found her. His brother's face had turned white. Cal understood the feeling, which told him more about how he felt about Mary than anything. "This cannot be a repeat of thirteen years ago," he spat. "I'm not going to watch another woman die, Roman."

He took off for the property, but Roman grabbed his pack and pulled him back.

"You can't run in there half-cocked, Cal!" Roman hissed into his ear. "We're surrounded by rocks. She could have snipers at the ready. You already know she was training them to kill. Use your head. We're of no use to Mina and Marlise if we're dead."

Cal took a calming breath and nodded, settling back against the wall as he listened to Marlise and Mina question Jen about The Miss. "Tread lightly, Marlise," he hummed, not wanting them to blow this operation before they had people in place to round up The Miss.

Roman leaned in when the mics went quiet. Marlise and Mina were in the pod now, and he had to hope they assumed it was wired for sound. "Let's head north. We're one klick south from where they stopped moving, according to the GPS."

One klick, Cal thought. A little more than half a mile separated them, but it felt like there was an ocean between them. Rather than speak, he nodded at Roman and headed north with his brother tight on his heels.

Chapter Nineteen

Marlise looked around the pod, surprised that it was clean and cool. There was a small efficiency kitchen in the middle and a bathroom, but the beds made a shiver run up her spine. There were two, one on each end of the pod, complete with a door that closed them off from the rest of the world. The bed behind the door was much bigger than necessary for one person, and the mountain of pillows, not to mention the mirrors on the ceiling, told the rest of the story.

Mina pulled her into the bathroom, turned on the shower and leaned into her ear. "I didn't see any obvious cameras, but that doesn't mean there aren't any. I would guess this place is bugged for sound." Marlise nodded, fear filling her now that they had found the woman who had already tried to kill them too many times. There was no way to know if help was coming or if Cal and Roman would find them in time.

They'd made sure to put on a show about how cool the pod was while Jen was with them. The more time they bought, the higher chance the guys would get to them before The Miss did. Before she left, Jen had told them to shower and dress in the new clothes left on the beds. Marlise had already noticed that the black T-shirt and pants were what Charlotte had described when explaining The Miss's new business plan. That was your welcome home outfit. Once The Miss decided where you'd be the most useful, you were given new clothes and a new identity. Marlise knew their disguises might fool the woman for a few moments, but their voices had probably already given them away. If not yet, they would once they stood in front of the woman.

"We're in trouble, aren't we?" Marlise asked, her voice wavering from fear.

"Stay calm," Mina ordered, leveling a brow at her. "Once we change, your tracker will be gone, but mine will remain. Roman and Cal will still be able to find us."

"That doesn't help us if we're already dead," she hissed, swallowing down her regret about agreeing to this mission. It was her idea, but now that she knew she was back in The Miss's grasp, the fear had taken over her courage.

"You have to keep your cool," Mina scolded. "Trust in Cal. He's not going to let you die in here. He loves you. You know that, right?"

"No, Mina, it's not like that," she insisted, even though she knew it was exactly like that. At least for her.

Mina put her finger to Marlise's lips. "It's been

like that since the day he met you. He will find a way to get us out. Besides, you know Roman isn't going to let The Miss have her way with me again."

That brought a smile to Marlise's lips, and she nodded once. "What's the plan then?"

"We stall as long as we can, and once it's dark, we get the hell out of here and hide."

"This entire property has to be under surveillance, Mina."

"Maybe, but the one thing I noticed on the way in is they run on generators. There's no power way out here. Chances are, there's minimal lighting once it's dark. All we have to do is avoid the guards and hole up until the authorities arrive."

Marlise finally nodded, but she knew there was no way they were getting out of this pod tonight unless it was by invitation from The Miss.

Roman took a knee and pointed ahead through the underbrush. "There are those tree cacti that Charlotte said lined the property."

Cal dropped down behind him and did a three-sixty search of the area around them. "They're big but not big enough to hide us from view. We need cover to reach out to Mack and find out how long until the authorities arrive."

"If they're arriving," Roman said. "We're practically on the border here, and I didn't see too many towns along the highway with a police force big enough to make a dent in this place."

Cal had thought the same thing on the way down, but Tucson wasn't that far away, and all they had to do was hold out long enough for the big guns to arrive. A skittering of rocks raised the hair on the back of his neck. Roman heard it too. He noticed him unsnap his holster, but Cal hoped they didn't have to resort to guns. The sound from a gunshot would travel for miles in a place like this, which would alert The Miss. She could kill Marlise and Mina before they were close enough to save them.

"No guns unless necessary," Cal whispered, and Roman nodded his understanding. "The sound was on our left. Could be wildlife."

Roman's sarcastic snort told him what he thought of that. The sun was setting, and they had to make a decision. They needed cover. Before Cal could move, there was a soft grunt, a thud and two more grunts before silence filled the desert again. Then came a sound that had never filled him with as much relief as it did today.

"Secure two, Mike," a voice said from their left.

Cal and Roman turned and scurried to a rock outcropping several yards to the west. When they reached it, Mack stood guard with a rifle while Eric tied up three women who were out cold.

"Mack, what the hell are you guys doing here?" Cal asked, trying to make sense of what he saw.

"Maybe you could show a little gratitude for us saving your unsuspecting butts from these three. They had you in their sights," Eric said, finishing with the zip ties. He stuffed gags in their mouths and dragged them behind some shrubs.

"I didn't like the idea of you two down here alone. Once you told me the women were going in, we headed down. The rest of the team is covering the clients while Selina keeps an eye on Charlotte. We have news," Mack said, crouching down. "We finally got The Miss's identity off that picture Marlise took."

"How?" Cal asked in surprise.

"Roman's people came through. Her name is Sofia Guerrero. Her father is Alejandro Guerrero."

"*The* Alejandro Guerrero? He's been suspected of running drugs and guns for years."

"One and the same," Mack agreed. "Turns out, he wanted to branch out and encouraged his daughter to continue his legacy across the border. Her mother was American, so she can come and go as she pleases."

"Is Alejandro involved in this compound?" Roman asked, his head motioning at the property east of them.

"That's less clear. No doubt he is, but we'd have to follow the paperwork."

"We'll leave that up to the authorities. Our only objective is to get our girls back safely. They're in a pod and waiting to be taken to The Miss. How far out are the authorities?"

"On their way from Tucson, but they're at least an hour out. They've been keeping an eye on the property, suspecting it was running drugs, but couldn't prove it. It didn't take much convincing to get them down here on a reported kidnapping."

"Do you have any idea how many armed guards are inside?"

"All we know is two at the gate. They're guards from Red Rye, according to Marlise."

"How do you want to handle this?"

"I want the innocents alive. I don't care if The Miss lives or dies, but I'd like there to be evidence left to prove she was behind the fire and the attacks on Marlise and Mina."

"Avoid setting anything on fire," Mack said with a grin. "Got it."

"My wife is in there," Roman said. "We need to get them out before the authorities arrive. I had hoped to get a confession out of The Miss, but confirmation that she's here is enough for me. We get the women out and let the police round up the rest of them."

All men nodded in agreement. "Eric and I will create a diversion at the front gate. What pod are Marlise and Mina in?" Roman showed Mack the tracker that had remained still for the last hour other than walking about the pod. "That's beneficial. They're on the west side of the satellite. We've already taken out those guards," Mack said, motioning at the women in the bushes. "This might be our only window to get them out before the cops arrive and the element of surprise is gone."

"We need ten minutes to get there, get them out and then to relative safety," Roman said, judging the distance to the pod on the map. "If things go bad, shoot your way out of it and get clear of the compound. We'll meet up at the large rock wall three klicks west."

"At which point we will discuss disobeying direct orders," Cal huffed.

Mack rolled his eyes. "Whatever. You're glad we're here. Give us five to get in place, and then we rock and roll."

His men took off, and Cal took a deep breath. He was glad they had come, but he would be happier when he had them out of that pod and The Miss in custody.

"I'm running point," Roman said in a way that told Cal not to argue. "You've got my flank."

"Every time, brother," he whispered, and then they headed for the cactus and two people who meant everything to them.

THE SUN HAD SET, making Marlise nervous as they waited for someone to get them. They'd been there for hours now, but Jen hadn't returned to the pod. Maybe they were going to wait until morning. Let them sweat it out for the night or see if they'd try to escape. They had already tried the door, and it was unlocked. They weren't trusting. They were self-assured. Girls who left a bad situation on the streets were going to be blinded by the comforts the pods had to offer.

"Hey!" a voice yelled, and Mina instantly stood up

from the chair by the table. There was more yelling and commotion, but it was a long way from their pod.

"The front gate?" Marlise asked, and Mina shrugged, her widening eyes reminding Marlise not to blow it.

"Who knows," Mina said with ease. Marlise could tell she wasn't at ease though. She was standing by the door of the pod listening to the yelling. "Who cares?"

There was a knock on the door, and Mina cut her gaze to Marlise, who rushed to her side before she opened the door. What she saw nearly brought her to tears.

"Secure two, Romeo," Roman whispered and motioned with his head to follow.

He didn't have to tell them twice. Marlise realized the commotion at the front gate was a diversion, and she prayed it wasn't Cal. She nearly fell to her knees when she saw him in a squat with his gun aimed into the darkness while he waited for them.

"Mack and Eric," Roman whispered as they ran toward Cal. "Authorities on their way."

That was all the information they would get as they were sandwiched between Cal in the front and Roman in the back. Cal hadn't so much as acknowledged her when he turned to motion for them to follow. She had to admit it hurt, but she understood he had a job to do. If he was going to get them out of this alive, he had to focus on nothing but the mission. The last time he split his focus, he lost Hannah. She tripped and nearly fell at the comparison. Roman righted her, but she could hardly breathe. They had to get out of this alive. Cal couldn't take losing another person he cared about in this life.

A shot rang out, and all four of them came to a halt as Cal held up a fist. The darkness was working against them now, and they couldn't see anything.

"Well, well, I've seen two ghosts as I live and breathe," a voice said from behind them. They turned in tandem just as a bright beam of light blinded them. When their eyes adjusted, The Miss stood before them flanked by two guards bearing guns. "Don't worry, my girls have already taken care of your men at the front gate. I'd love to chat, but first, I'll have to insist you lower your weapons and toss them over."

Roman held up his hands before he followed her orders, skittering the small pistol across the sand where the guard picked it up.

"You too," The Miss said to Cal. From the corner of her eye, Marlise watched him toss the gun behind him into the dark. "Did you think you could just waltz in here and take my girls after they'd just arrived? All the work I put into finding our perfect little witness, and it turns out, I should have just been patient."

"You can't kill us all," Mina said. "They'll never stop hunting you if they find us dead."

"Who said they were going to find you?" she asked. "You always were a little too by the book, Agent August, or is it Agent Jacobs now? I heard the happy news. Congratulations."

Marlise had a strong desire to punch this woman, but she bit her tongue to keep from aggravating her.

"We know who you are, Sofia," Cal said from behind her. "Is Daddy helping you keep the women hooked on heroin, so they'll stay and run drugs for you?"

"I don't need to hook them on drugs to get them to stay, right, girls?" she asked her guards, who nodded robotically.

Marlise knew drugs, and they were definitely on them.

"Is that why you had to put a tracker in them when you sent them out?" Roman asked. "Just in case they forgot their way back?"

"I would be a fool not to know where my assets are at all times."

"Sad that your team was so unsuccessful at Secure One."

"Were they though?" she asked in a voice that skittered fear down Marlise's spine. "From where I'm standing, I've been quite successful in procuring not one witness but two witnesses for the prosecution. Not that I care what happens to The Madame. She was a stepping stone to bigger and better things for me and my daddy. You four are the last thorn in my side, and then I can finally be free of her."

"The police know," Cal said. "They're on their way here."

"Doubtful," she replied with a reptilian smile.

"The police around here look the other way since my daddy funds their departments and their habits."

Marlise noticed the yelling at the front gate had ceased, and her heart sank. If what The Miss had said was true, then this was it for them. She would go to her grave without the chance to tell Cal she loved him. Part of her wanted to turn around and tell him, just take a moment before The Miss took her life, but fear froze her in place. Not of The Miss or of dying, but of the look on his face when he realized he would watch her die right before his demise.

"Girls, you know what to do." The Miss waved her hand at them. "Take out the trash." She turned just as a shot rang out.

"Cal!" she yelled, jumping to the side.

"Get down, Mary!" he screamed, and she dove to the ground, but not before she saw The Miss stumble backward, her body jerking left and then right. Cal threw himself over her as more shots rang out, and then there was silence for a moment before she heard the most welcome sound of her short life.

"Secure one, Charlie."

"Secure two, Romeo."

"Secure three, Whiskey."

"Secure four, Mike! You'll stay down if you're smart!" Mack yelled, probably at one of the guards. What was Mack doing here?

"Mary," Cal whispered, his voice filled with the pain and terror of the last five minutes.

"I'm okay," she promised, sitting up when he gave

her a hand, but he kept her face turned away from The Miss. "Are you okay?" She frantically patted him down, checking for bullet holes and blood.

He grabbed her hands and held them. "I'm okay, and I love you. I should have told you that two nights ago, but I convinced myself if I didn't say the words, I could pretend that wasn't the emotion in my chest every time I looked at you. I shouldn't have denied it though. My heart convinced me of that when I thought I was about to lose the woman I loved in the same horrible way as the last time."

"You didn't. I'm here, Cal. I'm here."

He pulled her into him and held her so tightly she couldn't breathe, so she sank into his warmth.

"I love you too, Cal. I have since the first day I was at Secure One, and you ordered everyone away and sat with me, helping me stay calm through the pain and terror no one else understood. That was when I knew you'd always be my only one, even if you sent me away."

"I'm not going anywhere, Mary, and neither are you. I'm always going to be here when you need me."

"Will you be here when I wake up?" she asked, the dots in front of her eyes making it hard to form words.

He held her out by her shoulders. "Wake up? What do you mean, baby?"

She gazed into his terrified eyes and smiled, running a finger down his cheek before it fell to her lap. "I couldn't let them take you from me, Cal."

"Roman!" Cal screamed as he rested her back on his lap and frantically searched for an injury. He found it and pressed his hand to her shoulder, the pain sparking a cry from her lips. "Roman! I need medical!"

Her vision dimmed, but she grabbed him and pulled him to her lips, kissing him until her body went slack and the darkness surrounded her.

Epilogue

"It's over," Marlise said, resting back against the head-rest of the SUV. "After all this time, she's finally out of our lives."

"I think she'll always be part of our lives. She brought me you, and I'll always be grateful for that," Cal whispered as he steered the car toward Secure One.

"To The Madame?" Marlise asked with surprise.

"To the universe. To whatever path you took to get here," Cal said with a shrug.

After three long months, the sentencing day for The Madame had finally arrived. They'd made the trip from Secure One to the Minneapolis courthouse to witness it with their own eyes. Cynthia Moore, aka The Madame, had been sentenced to twenty years in prison with no early release. She would be spending her time in Waseca while her husband, former special agent David Moore, spent his twenty years in Leavenworth just outside of Kansas City.

"Conjugal visits don't look promising," Cal said, trying not to laugh.

Marlise snorted at the thought and shook her head. "No, but they both got what they deserved, or they will once they're locked in with the general population."

The mastermind and her flunky would be in their seventies when they got out. If they didn't die behind bars, that is. Chances were good they wouldn't make it long once the other inmates learned who they were. They were initially facing life in prison, which would have been better in Marlise's opinion. Then The Miss died, and her secrets were revealed, so the prosecution offered them a plea deal to avoid another stay on the trial while they sorted through who was responsible for what in the sex trafficking ring. With The Miss dead, they were sure to find evidence, real or fake, proving The Madame had been the one to order girls to be killed for refusing to perform. If they could prove it, Cynthia was looking at life without parole, and she knew it, so pleading to twenty years in prison was an easy decision. It also meant Marlise and Mina didn't have to testify, which was a big relief.

The FBI never found the bodies of Emelia, Bethany or any of the other girls who had disappeared from The Miss's grasp. Where they were, no one knew, but Marlise suspected they were buried in the desert somewhere, or had been sold across the ocean to a land far away. Her heart ached at the thought of either situation. She wanted them found. The FBI assured her they were still looking, but they all knew the truth. The FBI wasn't going to waste resources on lost girls. The thought dampened her joy about the day a tad.

Cal turned the car down the driveway to Secure One as she pondered how it had only been a few hours since they'd left, but her whole life had changed again. Roman and Mina had headed back immediately after the sentencing while she and Cal had done some business in town that was long overdue. She finally had a legal name—Marlise Strong. She thought it was a bit too on the nose, but Cal said it was the perfect fit. She also had a social security card and a legal identification card. After nearly dying at the hands of The Miss twice, she was finally living.

Marlise had followed all the steps she needed to take to have a future. Each new accomplishment was a way to take back what everyone had taken away from her over the years. Her identity. Her passions. Her belief in herself. One man had a hand in giving her back all of those things, and today, he'd held her hand with a giant grin on his face when they'd presented her with a little card that promised a better life.

"I've given it a lot of thought. I'll do the interview for the book, but I'm not interested in the television or the public speaking events. I want people to learn about sex trafficking and the signs to watch for, but I prefer to be behind the scenes," Marlise said when the lights of Secure One came into view. She'd been offered so many opportunities to be an advocate for young women, and she wanted to help, but she didn't want to leave Secure One to do it.

Cal smiled, then shoulder bumped her after he'd parked the SUV below the lodge.

"What are you smiling about?"

"I'm just glad you aren't going to disappear from Secure One and my life to chase the Hollywood dream."

Marlise turned his chin to face her and kissed his lips. "I don't have a Hollywood dream, Cal. My dream is right here in this car," she whispered. "I love you."

"I love you too, Marlise Strong."

He climbed out of the car while she rubbed her right shoulder. It was sore after their long day, but it would be okay after she rested for the night. After surgery to remove the bullet from a guard's gun, she'd spent months doing physical therapy to strengthen it again. She hadn't considered that Cal was wearing a bulletproof vest and she wasn't. When she jumped in front of that bullet, it was a gut reaction to the threat against the man she loved. He'd saved her from The Miss, and it was her turn to do the same at that moment.

When he'd declared his love for her, he wasn't kidding, and he'd proven it every day for the last three months. He'd made sure she got the best care and therapy available and refused to let her do anything but rest and heal.

Cal helped her down from the car and linked his hand to hers. "How do you feel?"

"Free," she whispered.

"I only need that word to understand the emotion. It was the same emotion I felt in the fall when I let the past go and focused on my future."

"I feel like we should celebrate," she said as they walked into the lodge and toward the large dining room. It was where Marlise had found comfort those first few months she was at Secure One. Cal had put her in charge of cooking meals for his staff. That gave her a purpose and something to focus on besides her pain and trauma. There was something gratifying about seeing her friends enjoy something she made for their pleasure. Little by little, it had helped her regain her self-confidence and self-esteem.

"Funny you should say that," Cal said, motioning her into the dining room.

It was dark, so Marlise snapped the lights on, and everyone from Secure One jumped out and yelled, "Happy birthday!"

She turned to Cal with laughter on her lips when she leaned into him. "What's going on?"

"It's your birthday," Mina said from where she stood by Roman, a party hat on her head and a party blower in her mouth.

"Mina, my birthday is in January. You know that."

Cal kissed her cheek and gave her a wink. "We all know that, but when your ID came off the printer with today's date, I decided there was no better day to pick as your new birthday. Today we will celebrate the first birthday of Marlise Strong."

Marlise wiped away a tear as she accepted hugs from her friends and coworkers in the room. It was the final hug from Charlotte that pushed the tears over her lashes. Her friend was living through the same hell she had years ago, and she understood how hard it was to try and assimilate back into society when you were scared of everything. When they'd returned to Secure One after her surgery, Charlotte was still recovering from the infection in her leg, and Cal insisted she stay until she was healed. That would give her time to decide where she wanted to go and what she wanted to do. He'd suggested that she help in the kitchen since Marlise couldn't do a lot with one arm in a sling.

For the last three months, they'd worked together, but lately Marlise was spending more time in the control room learning the business of private security. She hoped that Charlotte would decide to stay and use Secure One as a safe place to heal and find herself.

"Did you make all this food?" Marlise asked after the hug.

"I did! It was fun, and Mack helped."

Marlise resisted the urge to glance at Cal. Mack spent a lot of time helping Charlotte, but no one said a word about it. She supposed Cal felt like it would be the pot and the kettle if he said anything to his friend about his devotion to the tiny, broken girl in the kitchen.

"Thank you. I know how much work it is. I appreciate you, Charlotte. When you're ready, say the word, and I'll help you find a new future."

Charlotte nodded and then motioned at the table. "We should eat before the food gets cold."

No one argued with her. They all took heaping plates of food back to the large tables to eat, chat, laugh and celebrate the end of a long case.

Cal stood up and walked to the middle of the room. "Mary," he said, motioning for her to join him. Abandoning her birthday cake, she walked toward him with a smile. He handed her a small package and motioned for her to open it. "I decided today was the perfect day for this."

Marlise opened the box and found a security badge every team member wore while working. "Secure One, Marlise Strong, client coordinator." She gazed up at him for an explanation. "Cal, what is this?"

"It's your new job. If you want it," he nervously added. "You've more than earned the right to that position. We all know you can do the job. Right, everyone?"

The room erupted in clapping and hooting as she lifted it from the box. "That means I'd have to give up the kitchen manager job."

"I think we've got that covered," Cal said with a wink at Charlotte, who smiled shyly.

"Then I'm ready," she agreed as everyone started clapping for her again. "Why does it say Bravo at the bottom?"

"Secure two, Romeo," Roman yelled.

"Secure three, Mike," Mack yelled.

"Secure one, Charlie," Cal whispered, and the meaning struck her.

"Secure four, Bravo," she called out with tears in her eyes. She hugged the badge to her chest. "Why Bravo? My name starts with *M*."

"Because I'm Charlie, and I'll follow you anywhere."

She threw her arms around him. "Thank you."

"No," he whispered. "Thank you for being mine. You are mine, right?"

"Always," she promised, accepting his kiss. "You never have to question my love for you or my dedication to the place that saved me."

"Then I have one more question to ask on your birthday, Marlise Strong." He pulled away from her and reached in his pocket, pulling out a ring that made her breath catch in her chest.

"Cal…"

"My sweet Mary," he said as he lowered himself to one knee and held up the ring. "I am so incredibly proud of you, do you know that?" he asked, and she nodded, her chin trembling with emotion. "You have come so far since we first met two years ago, and every day I stand in awe of your strength to make a difference in this world. To do good and spread love, even when you suffered at the hands of evil and hatred. I'm twice your size, but I know you're twice as strong. I know you just got that last name, and I'll respect it if you want to keep it, but today,

I hope you're willing to add mine to it as well. Will you marry me, Mary? Will you make your life here with me on this land and continue to make a difference in the fight against evil? Will you love me forever and give me the honor of being your husband?"

Marlise dropped to her knees and nodded, her eyes glistening with tears as he slipped the ring on her finger. "Nothing would make me happier than loving you forever, Cal Newfellow."

He captured her lips as their friends clapped and hooted. Someone turned the radio up, and everyone danced around them as they knelt with their lips and hearts connected. Cal helped her up, and Mina grabbed her in a hug, squeezing the daylights out of her in excitement.

"You deserve this," Mina whispered. "Enjoy every second of it. He loves you so much."

"Thanks, Mina," she said, just as the man in question pulled her back into his arms.

"Dance with me," he said, spinning her out and back into him, where he enveloped her with the length of his body to dance to a slow song on the radio.

"Breaking news alert," a voice said, as an alarm cut off the song. "The body of a young woman was pulled from the Red River today…"

Marlise pulled back and lifted a brow at her new fiancé. In return, Cal lifted one right back.

* * * * *

Don't miss the third book in
Katie Mettner's Secure One series when
The Red River Slayer *goes on sale next month!*

And if you missed the first title in the series,
Going Rogue in Red Rye County
is available now wherever
Harlequin Intrigue books are sold!

#2205 BIG SKY DECEPTION
Silver Stars of Montana • by BJ Daniels

Sheriff Brandt Parker knows that nothing short of her father's death could have lured Molly Lockhart to Montana. He's determined to protect the stubborn, independent woman but keeping his own feelings under control is an additional challenge as his investigation unfolds.

#2206 WHISPERING WINDS WIDOWS
Lookout Mountain Mysteries • by Debra Webb

Lucinda was angry when her husband left his job in the city to work with his father. Deidre never shared her husband's dream of moving to Nashville. And Harlowe wanted a baby that her husband couldn't give her. When their men vanished, the Whispering Winds Widows told the same story. Will the son of one of the disappeared and a writer from Chattanooga finally uncover the truth?

#2207 K-9 SHIELD
New Mexico Guard Dogs • by Nichole Severn

Jones Driscoll has spent half his life in war zones. This rescue mission feels different. Undercover journalist Maggie Caddel is tough—and yet she still rouses his instinct to protect. She might trust him to help her bring down the cartel that held her captive, but neither of them has any reason to let down their guards and trust the connection they share.

#2208 COLD MURDER IN KOLTON LAKE
The Lynleys of Law Enforcement • by R. Barri Flowers

Reviewing a cold case, FBI special agent Scott Lynley needs the last person to see the victim alive. Still haunted by her aunt's death, FBI victim specialist Abby Zhang is eager to help. Yet even two decades later, someone is putting Abby in the cross fire of the Kolton Lake killer. Scott's mission is to solve the case but Abby's quickly becoming his first—and only—priority.

#2209 THE RED RIVER SLAYER
Secure One • by Katie Mettner

When a fourth woman is found dead in a river, security expert Mack Holbock takes on the search for a cunning serial killer. A disabled vet, Mack is consumed by guilt that's left him with no room or desire for love. But while investigating and facing danger with Charlotte—a traumatized victim of sex trafficking—he must protect her and win her trust...without falling for her.

#2210 CRASH LANDING
by Janice Kay Johnson

After surviving a crash landing and the killers gunning for them, Rafe Salazar and EMS paramedic Gwen Allen are on the run together. Hunted across treacherous mountain wilderness, Gwen has no choice but to trust her wounded patient—a DEA agent on a dangerous undercover mission. Vowing to keep each other safe even as desire draws them closer, will they live to fight another day?

YOU CAN FIND MORE INFORMATION ON UPCOMING HARLEQUIN TITLES, FREE EXCERPTS AND MORE AT HARLEQUIN.COM.

HICNM0224

Get 3 FREE REWARDS!

We'll send you 2 FREE Books plus a FREE Mystery Gift.

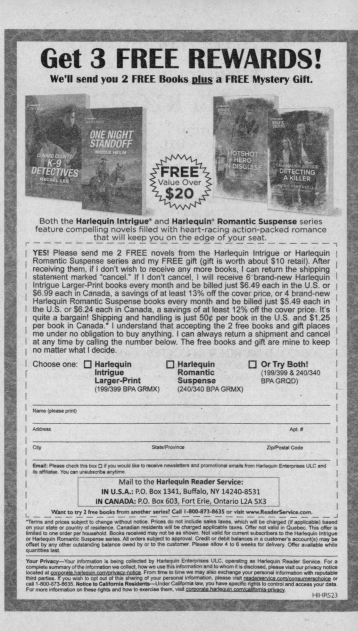

FREE Value Over **$20**

Both the **Harlequin Intrigue®** and **Harlequin® Romantic Suspense** series feature compelling novels filled with heart-racing action-packed romance that will keep you on the edge of your seat.

YES! Please send me 2 FREE novels from the Harlequin Intrigue or Harlequin Romantic Suspense series and my FREE gift (gift is worth about $10 retail). After receiving them, if I don't wish to receive any more books, I can return the shipping statement marked "cancel." If I don't cancel, I will receive 6 brand-new Harlequin Intrigue Larger-Print books every month and be billed just $6.49 each in the U.S. or $6.99 each in Canada, a savings of at least 13% off the cover price, or 4 brand-new Harlequin Romantic Suspense books every month and be billed just $5.49 each in the U.S. or $6.24 each in Canada, a savings of at least 12% off the cover price. It's quite a bargain! Shipping and handling is just 50¢ per book in the U.S. and $1.25 per book in Canada.* I understand that accepting the 2 free books and gift places me under no obligation to buy anything. I can always return a shipment and cancel at any time by calling the number below. The free books and gift are mine to keep no matter what I decide.

Choose one: ☐ **Harlequin Intrigue Larger-Print** (199/399 BPA GRMX)   ☐ **Harlequin Romantic Suspense** (240/340 BPA GRMX)   ☐ **Or Try Both!** (199/399 & 240/340 BPA GRQD)

Name (please print)

Address   Apt. #

City   State/Province   Zip/Postal Code

Email: Please check this box ☐ if you would like to receive newsletters and promotional emails from Harlequin Enterprises ULC and its affiliates. You can unsubscribe anytime.

Mail to the Harlequin Reader Service:
IN U.S.A.: P.O. Box 1341, Buffalo, NY 14240-8531
IN CANADA: P.O. Box 603, Fort Erie, Ontario L2A 5X3

Want to try 2 free books from another series! Call 1-800-873-8635 or visit www.ReaderService.com.

*Terms and prices subject to change without notice. Prices do not include sales taxes, which will be charged (if applicable) based on your state or country of residence. Canadian residents will be charged applicable taxes. Offer not valid in Quebec. This offer is limited to one order per household. Books received may not be as shown. Not valid for current subscribers to the Harlequin Intrigue or Harlequin Romantic Suspense series. All orders subject to approval. Credit or debit balances in a customer's account(s) may be offset by any other outstanding balance owed by or to the customer. Please allow 4 to 6 weeks for delivery. Offer available while quantities last.

Your Privacy—Your information is being collected by Harlequin Enterprises ULC, operating as Harlequin Reader Service. For a complete summary of the information we collect, how we use this information and to whom it is disclosed, please visit our privacy notice located at corporate.harlequin.com/privacy-notice. From time to time we may also exchange your personal information with reputable third parties. If you wish to opt out of this sharing of your personal information, please visit readerservice.com/consumerchoice or call 1-800-873-8635. **Notice to California Residents**—Under California law, you have specific rights to control and access your data. For more information on these rights and how to exercise them, visit corporate.harlequin.com/california-privacy.

HIHRS23